The SINFUL MAN

SHADE OF THE REAPER BOOK 3

KEITH ROMMEL

MILFORD HOUSE

an imprint of Sunbury Press, Inc.
Mechanicsburg, PA USA

MILFORD HOUSE

an imprint of Sunbury Press, Inc.
Mechanicsburg, PA USA

For information about special discounts for bulk purchases, please contact Sunbury Press Orders Dept. at (855) 338-8359 or orders@sunburypress.com.

To request one of our authors for speaking engagements or book signings, please contact Sunbury Press Publicity Dept. at publicity@sunburypress.com.

FIRST MILFORD HOUSE PRESS EDITION: August 2020

Set in Adobe Garamond | Interior design by Crystal Devine | Cover design by Lawrence Knorr | Edited by Jennifer Cappello.

Publisher's Cataloging-in-Publication Data
Names: Rommel, Keith, author.
Title: The sinful man / Keith Rommel.
Description: First trade paperback edition. | Mechanicsburg, PA : Milford House Press, 2020.
Summary: Alone, a troubled soul travels the Valley of Death, confronted by his sins.
Identifiers: ISBN : 1-978-620064-43-6 (softcover).
Subjects: FICTION / Thrillers / Psychological | FICTION / Psychological.

Product of the United States of America
0 1 1 2 3 5 8 13 21 34 55

Continue the Enlightenment!

To
James L. Perry
Lawrence Knorr
Tammi Knorr

Thank you for believing in my work.

1

THE FOREST

Present day.

"Get away from me!" Leo shouted and sprinted through the dense forest. Night had fallen and the bluish glow from the high moon sliced through breaks in the treetops like brilliant pillars of light. He used the beams to help navigate the unforgiving terrain that whipped past him. Swinging his gaze from left to right, the shadows that raced with him kept perfect pace and intensified his worry.

"What do you want from me?" he shouted. His voice cracked and sounded pathetic.

Picking up speed, he recklessly plowed through the overgrowth and tumbled blindly down an embankment concealed by the gloom. Head over feet he rolled down the steep slope and crashed into a fallen tree at the base of the hill. Coming to a sudden and complete stop, his head snapped back, banging into the wood, his breath forced from his lungs. He saw stars and the twilight spun; his right shoulder throbbed in pain.

Crack!

All around him the unmistakable sound of sticks snapping came from the thick tangle of turbid green, brown, and black. Then the wheeze of many things that breathed heavily, as if they were tired from their run, gathered. A feeling of malevolent peril forced him to focus and made him stand, but his body trembled in protest. Exhausted and gasping for air, he fell again.

"Why are you after me?" he struggled to say, his forehead and nose pressed into the dirt. His mind told him to flee but he couldn't get his body to cooperate. The beat of his heart slammed inside his chest and threatened to break out of its bone cage.

Then, as if in response to his question, laughter from a hundred different voices boomed all around him and developed into a chorus of malice.

"What is it you want from me?" he whimpered.

Desperate to escape the pack that hunted him, he ignored the headache and stabbing pain in his shoulder and clawed the moist earth. As he pulled his body through wet leaves and rotting woodland, the approaching footfalls from the wicked that closed in on him vibrated the ground.

"Run," the sinister voices said. The word was a disturbing whisper spoken from dozens of lips that felt as though they were pressed against his ear.

The instinct to survive made Leo forget about his ailments and exhaustion and he got up and scurried through a narrow path carved in the forest. The overgrown vegetation slapped at his legs and face and stung his skin. His lungs burned and the overwhelming desire to stop was overruled by the intense fear of being caught by whatever it was that chased him.

He entered a small clearing and spotted a lopsided wooden shack with no windows that was tucked neatly away in a clump of foliage. He almost ran by it because the vegetation that wrapped its aging shell disguised it well, but at the last minute it had gained his attention. It was as if it had beckoned him.

"Hello?" he said with hope, his eyes bulging and unblinking as if what he saw would disappear if he lost sight of it for even a second.

A puff of smoke that escaped its dilapidated chimney meant someone had to be home and they would provide him with protection from his unyielding pursuers.

"Help!" he thoughtlessly dared to shout and hurried to the crooked door. Trying the handle was fruitless; the lock on the inside jiggled but held.

"Please, help me!" he said and lifted both arms to hit the door. Cringing and groaning from the powerful piercing sensation in his injured shoulder, he used his foot to kick the pathetic door. It was surprisingly tough and he waited impatiently, distracted by his pain and the rustling in the verdure all around him.

"Hurry up!" he screamed, his voice cracking with the strain.

Latches slid away and the door opened a pinch. He stepped forward and suddenly everything around him became eerily quiet as if nothing were ever after him. About chest height, an eye stared back at him and studied him for a moment.

"What do you want?" the scratchy voice of a female said.

"Someone is after me and I'm lost," he said, exhausted and fraught. "You've gotta let me inside!"

He pushed the door but it slammed into something on the inside and stopped, keeping him outside.

"You bang on my door and attempt to bring your troubles into my house? Then you try and force your way inside?"

"Please, you've gotta let me in!"

"Go on, scat! I don't want your troubles becoming my own," the woman said and slammed the door shut.

The things in the forest came alive again and the hair on the back of his neck stood. Desperate to escape whatever it was that had followed him, he forgot about his pain and beat the door with his fists.

"Open the goddamn door or they're going to get me!"

The hinges whined and a short plump old woman in a flowery nightgown stepped outside. She held a shotgun and had it trained on Leo's face.

"Don't you dare use the Lord's name in vain around my house, boy." Her teeth were missing and her lips curled in around the gums.

"I'm sorry," he said and backed away, raising his hands. "I didn't mean anything by it. I'm not here to cause you any trouble or disrespect you in any way." He looked over his shoulder, nervous. "And if you could be so kind to allow me inside, I would hope I could use your phone and call for some help."

She moved the muzzle of the gun close to his face, closed an eye, and looked down the sight centered between Leo's eyes. "Don't you move a muscle, do you understand me? Just because I'm old doesn't mean I don't know how to squeeze this trigger here. Believe me, I don't mind spreading your face all the way into them trees back there."

"I ain't gonna move," Leo said as sweat ran down his face and itched his chin. He wanted to wipe it away but didn't dare move.

The old lady stood motionless and watched the woodsy perimeter out of the corner of her eye. The darkness and eerie light of the moon collided and cast her wrinkled face in a sinister way. Scrunched and formed into a permanent expression of annoyance, she lifted her chin and sniffed the air.

"Who do you suppose is after you?" she said and eyed him for a moment. Her distrust was easy to see and her pointer finger hugged the trigger.

"I don't know," he said. "I didn't see their faces. But I could hear them and they were all around me."

"Mmmhmm."

"Please loosen up your grip around that trigger. I'm not going to do anything and I don't need you accidentally shooting me."

She glanced around the tree line with the gun held at the ready.

"Well," she said, and relaxed some. "I think you've lost them. If you want, you can come along inside. You look like you've been through hell." She motioned him along with a subtle shake of the shotgun.

"Thank you," Leo said, and without delay he moved inside the cabin.

A brick fireplace built into the back wall illuminated the small sized room and revealed details of the old warped plank boards pitted with knots. A cast iron cauldron was suspended over the flames and an oak table with two chairs was positioned approximately five feet away from the fire. Atop the table was a closed worn book twice as thick as the bible, and a long red tassel hung out of the pages.

Immediately to his right was a long, dimly-lit hallway that dead-ended at a closed door. A piece of paper was attached to the door and the ends drooped, helping to conceal a message that was difficult to decipher at this distance. The firelight that played with shadows barely had enough strength to reach that far.

The woman engaged the thick metal deadbolts located slightly above her head and at her ankles. They whined and clicked as they slid into place.

She set the butt of the gun into a dimple on the floor, leaned it against the wall, and looked at Leo.

"Look at you," she said, and shook her head. "You're a mess."

Leo looked at himself. Mud stained his clothes and debris clung to him. Clumps of dirt surrounded his shoes and continued to shed from his garments as his limbs trembled uncontrollably. His head, neck, and shoulder hurt something awful, sending waves of pain deep into his back.

"Sit down before you track that muck you rolled in all over my house," she said. "Besides, I don't need you falling over in the middle of my floor. I don't have the strength to pick you up and you've already given me enough work by having to clean this mess up."

Leo looked behind himself and at the dirt trail. "I'll clean it," he said and wobbled.

She reached to assist him but he managed to steady himself.

"I don't need your help. You can barely stand," she said. "Now do as I say and go and sit."

Leo moved to the chair and plopped himself down, sapped of strength. The tremble in his body intensified and his teeth chattered. The old woman watched him for another moment before she shook her head and shuffled into a room to the right of the fireplace. It was dark and he hadn't noticed it until this moment. It immediately repelled him as if the things that were outside were in there, behind the veil of obscurity, hiding from the firelight and waiting to reach out and drag him into oblivion.

He stood fast and backed away, needing to create more space, unsure how long their arms might be. The old woman reentered the room with a slight bend in her back and a mild limp that made her left foot clop on the floor. She carried a soiled blanket and tossed it at him.

"Sit back down and get a hold of yourself."

The blanket stunk but he didn't care. Pulling it over his shoulders, he wrapped it around his body and gave into a powerful shiver. Whether that was from the cold that settled in his bones or the fear from his ordeal, he didn't know.

"Is that better?" she asked.

"Much." He nodded. "Thank you."

He looked around the room and noticed there weren't any light switches on the walls or light fixtures hanging from the ceiling. There were no windows and nothing decorated the walls. Everything was made of wood and it creaked.

"It has provided me with shelter for a long time."

"What?" Leo said, her words bringing him back to her.

"You're looking around as if you're repulsed by what you see."

"No, that's not it, and I'm sorry I gave you that impression. I was just looking around, trying to make sense of where I am and what this place is."

"It's my home."

It may have been her home, but there was a heavy feeling about it. It was hard to describe and something he didn't want to discuss with the strange old woman for fear of insulting her. "Do you have a phone I can use?"

"Don't be silly," she said and laughed.

"If you allow me to use your phone I could be on my way."

"There is no phone."

"How do you not have a phone?" He looked around some more. "You're in the middle of nowhere."

She flashed a smile. "I am in the middle of somewhere."

"Where?"

"Right here," she said and patted the tabletop. "That's all you need to know right now."

"I should go. Is there a back door I can use?"

"That's not a good idea. You're not thinking clearly. You're chilled and you suffered trauma. Where do you think you're going to go in your condition and with them outside?"

She was right. He was hurt and weak and couldn't argue with her logic.

"Sit down like I told you and keep yourself covered with that blanket. If you think you're shaking now, wait until your adrenaline rush subsides. You're going to feel like you're freezing and I don't want to hear you complaining about it. Especially if you're not going to listen to me."

Leo hesitated.

"Help yourself for once and listen to reason," she said. "Go on, take a load off and face the fire. It'll help you get the chill out of your bones."

"But didn't you hear anything I said to you?" Leo said. The sense of terror was overwhelming, so why wasn't she concerned? "People were chasing after me and you're talking about me sitting in front of a fire to get warm? What do I do about them?" He pointed at the door.

"What do you think you should do?"

"Call for help."

"Even if I had a phone, there is no one you can call."

"But there has to be someone," he protested.

"There isn't," she said, her words as cold as the wet that settled into his bones. They were uncaring and seemingly bothered by his worry.

He looked at the shotgun.

"I want you to think back," she said. "How did you get in the forest?"

"I don't know," he whispered, and sat heavily. "The people outside were relentless and have been chasing me. I couldn't see where I was going and I tumbled down this hill. I smashed my head and shoulder into a fallen tree." He tried to lift his arm but awakened the pain in his shoulder. Shrinking in his seat, he writhed.

"Those aren't people that were chasing after you," she said.

He stiffened, forgetting about his agony. "What do you mean they aren't people?"

"It is exactly as I said. They're not people."

"But . . . I could hear their footsteps and their voices. How could you say they aren't people?"

"Ahh, it doesn't matter." She pulled at her chin. "I don't suppose us talking about it will help you right now anyways. I don't see the sense in getting you all worked up any more than you already are. And as long as you mind yourself, you can stay a while. You'll be safe for the time being."

"Safe? In here?" He looked around the room. He settled his worried gaze on the fire and let out a nervous laugh. "This shack is made of wood and all they need to do is burn it down!"

She shook her head and the loose skin on the underside of her chin swayed. "They wouldn't dare think to do that. We have an understanding."

"An understanding? Do you know who they are?"

7

She busied herself with the fire, shifting the logs with a poker. The embers raced up the chimney. "What difference does it make if I know who they are?"

"Because if you do then they might have led me here to you on purpose."

She rested a moment. "If that were true, then that would mean you were trapped. So I could ask you what the point is in concerning yourself with things you have no control over. You are safe right now, isn't that enough?"

"I don't know," he said, and the voice in his head told him to flee while he still had the chance.

"Besides, this old shack is built like a fortress and it has provided countless others with a safe place to put their heads for a night. You should be thankful, not looking for flaws."

"I am," he said but found no comfort in her words. He was consumed with so many questions that he couldn't organize his thoughts enough to ask them.

"I hope so," she said and faced him. Her hair was pinned up and was so gray it looked white. The gown she wore was worn, making the fabric sheer in some spots. Her hairy shins made him shrink; although he knew woman grew hair on their legs and underneath their arms, it was alarming to see it. Slippers that were as worn as the gown barely fit her swollen purple feet. Gnarled toes hung over the ends of the slippers and the discolored nails touched the bare wood floors and made a scraping sound.

"None of this makes any sense," he said and ran stiff fingers through his hair. "I don't even know what the hell I'm doing here."

"Have you thought to keep your mouth closed long enough to allow yourself some time to figure it out?"

He shook his head. Silence wasn't what he needed. "All I can remember is being chased—"

"Yeah, I already know that." She waved a dismissive hand. "You told me that outside and then you said it again when we got inside. You need to quiet yourself."

"I can't. Look," he said and held out a trembling hand. "Especially not after what I just went through."

"Maybe I should give you some tea." She grumbled something to herself that he couldn't hear. "Yeah, I think the tea will help you relax and get rid of the edge."

She removed a ladle off of a hook that hung next to the fireplace and shuffled to the cauldron.

"What are the chances that those were wild animals that were after me?" he said.

She looked over her shoulder. "You don't think I could possibly have an understanding with a pack of wild animals, do you?"

She scooped hot water and carefully filled a mug before she set it down in front of Leo.

"If those aren't animals, then who are they?" he said.

"You're not asking the right questions, Leo. I don't think you mean who, but rather, what," she said.

A slow, all encompassing sense of panic closed in on him and he needed to get away.

"But don't be troubled over the details right now. It won't change a thing and it can wait a while." She tapped her fingernail on the side of the mug and refocused his waning attention. "Drink up while it's still warm. You're still shivering and it'll help get the chill out of your bones, too."

He wanted to decline the offer but needed something to help get the chill out. "Thank you," he said, and the aroma dismissed all of his worries.

"It looks like you're going to be here for a while so I might as well help you relax. I really can't take the way you're so fidgety."

She returned the ladle to its proper place and nudged the mug towards him. "Come now, drink up. Like the fire, it'll help you feel better," she said, and for the first time since his arrival, he saw a gentleness about her.

The aroma of evergreen filled his nose and he wrapped his hands around the warm, steaming mug. It reminded him of the holidays and it opened him to her offering. With a sip, the warmth flowed down his throat and helped reduce his anxiety.

She sat at the table across from him and a pleasant, unwavering grin took over her face.

"How are you feeling?" she said.

"Amazingly better."

"And to imagine how frightened you were only a short time ago."

"You're right," Leo said. "It is peaceful here and I feel safe."

"When you first arrived, I could see and feel your fear and your resistance to listen to what I was trying to tell you. I want you to know that you are safe here, but you won't be allowed to stay too long so use your time wisely."

"I understand," Leo said, his face hovered over the warm mug as he sniffed the scent.

"Now let's get you out of those clothes so I can clean and dry them. When you undress, leave them on the floor where you are. Now go on, I won't look."

She turned her back to him. Though she was small and feeble, the stare of someone that had lived a long, tough, and lonely life remained long after she looked away.

He couldn't look past the fact that she opened her home to him. And because of that, he couldn't help but respect her wishes of wanting to keep her home clean and giving him fresh clothes to wear. He stood and stripped to his underwear, his filthy clothes stacked in a sloppy heap where he stood. He bent to pick them up.

"That's a nasty gash you got there," she said.

Leo dropped the clothes and grabbed the blanket and struggled to cover himself.

"You need to look at it," she said.

Leo looked at the gash and it was long across his abdomen and trickled blood. The skin was wet and soiled with mud, hiding the details. There was no pain so he shrugged.

"I must've gone through a thorn bush or something." He wrapped his body with the blanket and sat.

"I'll get these soaking in a tub. I'll be right back." She took the clothes away.

A shiver shook Leo's body and he faced the fire. The consuming feeling of dread began to abate and he was glad to be inside the cabin and in front of the blaze. The heat was comforting and he held his shaking hands out as if to capture the warm air in the palm of his hands.

Dried dirt clung to every inch of his flesh and was wedged underneath his fingernails. Lacerations on his forearms bled, too, and the shoulder that had crashed into the log made him grimace. The crackling hardwood flames told him that the worst was behind him now and that he was going to be all right.

"That should help loosen the grime up," she said, emerging from the dark room.

Ripped from his reverie, Leo flinched.

She laughed gently. "You scare easily."

"I'm sorry. I was deep in thought," he said, and tried to return to the place of tranquility and peace, but her sudden return frightened him so that his heart pounded furiously.

Turning away from the fire and resting his elbows on the table, he rubbed his eyes with the heels of his hands. "I was watching the flames dance and it was really captivating. It is amazing how mesmerizing they can be. And you were right. The warmth is invigorating and it has made me feel alive again."

She sat across from him. "I often hear how people don't slow down enough to look around and appreciate the smaller details. Those details are what hold the beauty in life," she said. "It is all around them, but they just don't care enough to see it. And usually when they do, it's too late for them."

Leo turned towards the fire again and raised his hands and lifted his chin. "Well this right here is beautiful and I appreciate it."

"You should know that your time is done here when the last log burns out," she said, prompting Leo to look at the small stack of about ten logs.

"I've lit many fires in those bricks there, hoping someone would be delivered from the darkness. But I know that isn't possible and I shouldn't talk about it."

As he stared at the fire, the darkness she spoke of was kept at bay.

"Leo?" she said and reached her hands across the table, inviting his touch. He placed his hands into hers. Speckled with age spots, her hands were soft and gentle, concealing great strength. He looked into her sad eyes and she stared back at him.

"I wish you knew how strong you were," she said.

He looked back at the fire, puzzled.

"But you gave in. Why?"

He looked at her and her eyes held onto the question, waiting for an answer he couldn't give.

"Why do people give up so easily?" she said. "I need to understand that."

Her gaze bore a hole into his receding comfort but the answers to her questions were far away, masked by the drink.

"What did I give into?" he said and tried to remember. Everything about this moment was a struggle. His memory started at the chase and anything before that was a blank.

She rubbed his hands with a gentle stroke of her thumbs and with a soft voice said, "I want you to die."

He pulled his hands away, her words like a forceful slap, her touch suddenly cold.

"What did you just say to me?"

She glowered, her expression twisted into something awful. He stood and was uncertain if being locked inside the cabin with this crazy old woman was any better than being outside with the things that chased him.

"Why do those words frighten you so?"

"Because I don't know why you would say that to me."

"You really don't remember, do you?"

He shook his head. "I'd like my clothes back."

"Oh, honey, you didn't find this place by accident. The forest. Those things outside. They're all here for you."

"I really need to go."

Scratching sounds on the outside of the cabin walls moved slowly and hinted at ill intent. It silenced his protest and he listened to it pick up in intensity. Someone—something scratched at the door and there was a relentless desire to get at him.

"Is that them?" he said and hid beneath the table.

"I suppose it is."

"What do they want?"

"You."

"Why?"

"Sit down with me and face your fears or you can go outside and find out why they're here for yourself."

The scratching stopped and Leo looked at the door.

Bang!

The door rattled and Leo recoiled.

"What the hell was that?" he said and scooted away. The intense heat of the flames emanating from the fireplace was like the breath from something evil panting behind him, but he didn't care. His eyes remained firmly on the door, convinced whoever was there would break through.

"Oh, that?" she said and laughed. She gave the table a gentle pat. "Let them make their noise and let us finish our tea. You're safe inside the cabin and we can spend a little time getting to know each other. Don't you think that would be nicer than having to face them?"

2

THE HUNGER

The past.

A sudden crack of thunder woke Leo. He occupied a place devoid of any light—the perfect depiction of what his life had become. He needed a moment to think where he might be because a stairwell, a stranger's apartment, or even an obscure alleyway had served as his bed most nights.

"Hello?" he said, and his voice echoed in the small space.

A distant flash of lightning gave him a snapshot of his surroundings. He was at home and was fully dressed, lying on top of dirty clothes and junk used as a makeshift bed. Stretching and trying to ignore the deep hunger pain that angrily rolled around in the pit of his belly, he stood. His body trembled in protest—a feeling he should have grown accustomed to by now but hadn't. He battled the way he felt only to do it again the next day. Balancing by pressing his hands against a wall, he leaned forward and waited for a wave of nausea to pass.

As he felt his way around, things that were scattered across the floor entangled his feet and slowed his pace. Locating the light switch, he flipped it and the click offered him nothing. The room remained dark as if it wanted to conceal what he had become.

"Damn," he said and moved the toggle switch up and down over and over again with no change.

The forceful pitter-patter of falling rain tapped the small window like an incessant poke from stiffened fingers that purposely tried to draw his attention. Another rumble of thunder made way for a series of lightning flashes and the window well that was partially filled with leaves blocked most of his view but he could see the raging storm outside. Strong winds blew the rain sideways and carried more leaves into the window well.

Looking away from what he saw, the irony wasn't lost on him. The chaos that roiled around outside was similar to what was going on inside him.

He patted his pockets and removed a brass Zippo lighter, pulled open the hinge top, and turned the flint wheel with his thumb. Sparks ignited the gas and gave him light.

The muted glow of the small flame illuminated the studio apartment and hinted at the unsuitable conditions of his subsidized living space. Broken drywall exposed the wall studs and frayed electrical wires. Active water stains on the ceiling came from leaking pipes—the messy, jobless tenants above that cared nothing for the space they inhabited. Weeds grew out of the cracks in the concrete floor and he often watered them as if they were decorative plants to be cared for.

Unable to remember the last time he watered the weed at his feet, he knelt and examined it. Satisfied it was still alive, his focus shifted to the outline of a body carved into the concrete floor. He felt an attachment to it and studied it a moment, but didn't know why. The figure was bent in a way that suggested that the final moments of life were horrible for this person so he touched it with the intention of comforting it.

"Do you like your flower?" he asked and stroked the head as if it had hair.

The weed had grown soon after he made the outline, inspired by an event he fought to forget but struggled to remember. He had spent many nights tracing it, trying to get it right but certain it was wrong. Still, night after night he dug the impression further into the slab as his mind descended further and further into a place people didn't come out of.

"Well, whoever you are, I hope your pain is gone," he said and stood. "Mine follows me wherever I go."

He turned away with the knowledge that the night would be much easier if he didn't dwell on what he couldn't change, but rather focused on what he needed to get done to help him survive into the next moment.

Half eaten food scraps discarded on top of the rubbish he had collected off of the streets drew his attention and reminded him of the ache in his stomach. "I'm hungry," he said, unable to remember the last time he took nourishment.

Although the stink of neglect had fouled the air, it had become unnoticeable to him and didn't interfere with his hunger.

Patting his waist out of habit, he realized he was missing something. "Where did I put my bag?"

Forgetting about his appetite, he held the lighter up high and searched the room. Locating his bag on top of an overturned appliance box used as a piece of furniture, he made his way to the cardboard box, pausing several times along the way to wait for the nausea to go away. When he picked up the waist pack, he almost dropped it. Heavy and awkward, he buckled it, positioning it comfortably just above his protruding hipbones where it sagged. Next, he grabbed his hoodie, which was folded into a perfect square, shook it open, and put it on.

Gurgle.

"Yeah," he said, and gave his slim waistline a hard slap. "I hear you and I'm working on it. I have some things to figure out so give me a second, would you?"

But another ache pushed itself past the hunger pain and made itself known. It was powerful and consuming and instantly made him sweat, demanding every bit of his attention.

"I don't know how, but I'll take care of you, too," he said. "Leave me be and let me get something to eat first."

As if in response to his protest, a powerful pain in the pit of his belly bent him over and he slammed his eyes shut and clenched his fists. Sweat beaded on his forehead and his lips were pulled back in a tight grimace as he fought the gut wrenching ache.

"I said I would take care of you, too." He shook and the sweat dripped off of his nose and he grabbed his gut. "Lighten up, I'll do it!"

At those words, the symptom eased. Careful not to right himself too quickly, he rose and held out the lighter and looked around the room. Moldy pieces of bread leftover from a sandwich he couldn't remember eating tempted him. To get rid of one burden so he could begin working on the next seemed like the best plan.

He fingered the scraps, but the stale bread was like a rock. He tongued his teeth, weighing his options. They rocked painfully in the weakening grip of his diseased gums. Unsure if his teeth could compete against the hardness of the stale bread, he tossed the scraps aside.

Gurgle.

"I can't eat that," he reasoned and pulled the hood over his head and sunk deep into the shadow of the fabric. It was safe there and he liked it.

The lights blinked on and he recoiled. Shading his eyes with his forearm, he wished the electricity had remained off because the darkness was so much more desirable.

Gurgle.

"Yeah, I know, I'm going," he said and extinguished the flame to his precious lighter and made his way to the door. Exiting the apartment, he met the rainfall driven by a powerful wind and was determined to tame his hunger. A flash of pain served as a reminder and made him wince.

"I said I'll take care of you both."

His eyes moved to his feet so he could avoid the moist onslaught that was being driven by a powerful squall. Defying the storm, he began his journey.

3

A NEW GUEST

Present day.

Leo crawled out from underneath the table, his eyes firmly on the door.

"I think they've made their point," the old woman said.

Wham, wham, wham!

The floorboards squeaked underneath Leo's feet as his eyes swept across the ceiling. Someone was running around up there and they were moving fast.

"You need to ignore them and sit down," she said.

"I don't want to sit," he said and continued to follow the sound of the footfall moving around the roof. "I want to get out of here."

"Now, you and I both know you can't go out there."

"It's like they're waiting out there, knowing I'm going to come when that fire dies."

The old woman smiled.

"I'm trapped," Leo said.

"So do as I suggest and sit."

"But if I were to make a run for it right now, I might catch them off guard. I mean, they're probably expecting me to stay until those logs are gone. Maybe I could get a big enough lead that I could lose them in the dense woodlands."

"They have strength in numbers," she said. "But for you, there is power in knowledge. Now, come and sit. We have a lot to talk about."

Leo remained still, trapped by indecision.

"Come on," she said and tapped the tabletop with her fingernails.

He looked at her with wavering trust.

"Fool," the old woman said and looked away from him. "You just stand there looking stupid, wasting what little precious time you have left with me."

She shuffled to the stack of firewood and grunted as she bent to add a log to the fire.

"We're down to nine now," she said, and embers rushed up the chimney. The wood crackled and popped as it reluctantly accepted the fiery lick of flame. "Suppose I was to open that door and force you outside. Do you think that would help you make a decision?"

Leo shook his head. "I just need a moment to think about things. I'm trying to figure out where I am and how I got here."

"The answers you seek are right here for you to discover. To get them, all you have to do is sit at this table and have a conversation with me."

"I can't sit."

"Well, why not?"

The sound of running feet overhead made him watch the ceiling again.

"Are you afraid of them?"

"I'm just . . . confused."

"You're scared. I can see it."

"OK, yes, I'm scared, too, OK?"

"As you should be, Leo." She lifted her chin and looked into his eyes. Squinting, she said, "But not as bad as you're going to be once that fire dies."

He shivered. "Why do you say things like that?"

Her wide smile exposed her toothless gums. "Because you need to know they're dangerous. You can't just run past them and think they won't be able to keep up. Besides, they can sense your fear like I can and they know you're not going out there. No matter how bad you want to, you won't. Once you see that darkness staring you in the face, you're going to want no part of it. This is what you need—" she pointed at the fire— "It'll keep you safe. And most of them have gone back into the trees and are resting. You should be taking advantage of the opportunity to learn as much as you can, but the foolish have always thought they were too smart to take the advice of another."

"This is madness," he whispered and looked around the room. Vines had infiltrated the interior of the cabin. Blended into dark joints and seams where boards met, the flicker of the firelight revealed the leafy vine in brief snapshots. "I couldn't possibly rest here. Things are too weird."

"The meaning of this place is so profound and carries such a sadness that it could only be lost on someone like you."

Maybe that's what that black room had inside it. Sadness.

"And regardless of how badly you'd like to defy what is going on here, it will play out exactly as it is supposed to. You will give in to your resistance and look to satisfy your need to know."

Those words were true. He could feel the pull.

"I understand you're frightened and you have a million questions racing through your head. But I don't want you to waste your time or energy on the things that don't matter anymore," she said. "This will come, and by this time tomorrow you won't have the luxury of this shelter. So heed my words, smarten up and make use of your time here."

A sudden loud barrage of knocks jounced the thick barrel bolts and Leo jumped, facing the door.

"I thought you said they had gone away!" he shouted.

"That isn't them, Leo."

Bang, bang, bang!

At the second barrage of knocks he ran down the hallway to the door at the end. He tried the handle but it was locked. Lifting the sagging edges of the paper that was hanging on the door, he read: Keep out!

The note had been written in crayon by the hand of a child.

"What is this place?" Leo said and whimpered.

Another series of bangs came from the front door and Leo was frantic to escape it. Trying the handle again, he squeezed the lever with both hands as hard as he could and was dropped to a knee from the jolt of pain from his shoulder.

Bang, bang, bang!

Certain the group was making their move to get him, he pressed his back against the wall and waited for them with a fierce pounding heart.

"Please, let me inside," a muted voice from outside called. It penetrated the interior of the cabin. Fright and desperation were easy to hear in the words, changing Leo's need to flee into that of wonder and even concern.

"Hello?" Leo said and stood. He emerged from the hallway with his eyes fixated on the door.

"Hello? I can hear you, can you hear me?" the muted voice called back.

"Yes, I can hear you!" Leo shouted back and looked at the old woman. She winced as she settled into the seat, seeming unmoved by the visitor.

"Aren't you going to see who this is?"

She shook her head. "I'm not getting up again. My back hurts something terrible." Her body crumpled over as she leaned heavily on her elbows.

"But you have to help him!"

"No, I don't."

"But they're after him, too!"

"So, what am I supposed to do, save the world?"

"Open the door and let him inside!"

"Why would I invite someone else in when I can't even get you to listen?"

The door rattled. "Come on man, open the damn door!" the man outside shouted. "Someone is after me! I can hear them all around me."

"You've got to let him inside!" Leo said. "Please."

The old woman sat there, consumed by her pain.

"Didn't you hear me?" he said. "Those things are after him, too!"

"Yeah, I heard you, and so what? I don't want his troubles becoming my own. I've already managed to take on yours and I'm not happy about it."

"Well, if you don't let him in, I will." Leo looked at the gun and thought to take it and use it.

"You don't even know who is at the door," she said and shook her head. "Maybe it is one of them pretending to be someone in distress."

Leo paused. "No, you said it yourself that it's not them. Besides, his fear is real, I can hear it. I know because it's exactly how I felt."

"So you say. Go ahead and open that door then. When they snatch you and drag you outside, I'm not going to help you and you'll never get away. You've managed to allow strangers to cause you enough trouble. It would behoove you to mind your business this time," she said and sat back, her displeased face unable to hide her battle with physical pain. "Whoever that is out there, they don't deserve your compassion."

"How can you say that?"

"Because that's the way it is, Leo. There is no other reason."

"I know what it's like out there and it's as scary as hell. Let him inside and we'll sort everything else out afterwards."

Three heavy thumps on the door increased Leo's frustration.

"Open the damn door!" the man outside said. It sounded like his lips were pushed close to the doorjamb. "You can't just leave me out here with them. Please, I'm begging you."

"Why are you just sitting there?" Leo growled at the old woman. "Get up and help him!"

The old woman sighed. "All right already! But, before I can let him inside, I need you to sit here with me."

"Why? Just let him in!"

Thump, thump, thump.

"Because it is important that you don't see who has come."

He looked at the door and then at the old woman. "Why, who is he?"

"Someone that doesn't concern you," she said. "You wanted me to let him in and your stalling is preventing that. Tick tock, Leo. If you don't do what I say, I'm not going to let him in."

Leo sat.

She cupped her hands around her mouth. "Keir," she shouted, her voice booming. "Your guest has arrived and I think he's had enough for now. Why don't you come out of your room and let him in?"

Leo heard the sound of a door opening and looked over his shoulder to see a pale child no older than five years of age emerge from the hallway. Wearing black shoes laced high up to the shins, striped stockings, and a plain dress, freckles dotted the palest of cheeks. Leo stared, trying to decipher whether it was a boy or a girl.

"Are you ready?" the child said, the voice revealing him to be a boy.

"Why is he dressed like that?" Leo said.

"That was his favorite era. He thinks people should learn lessons from when times were much simpler and I tend to agree. Don't you think he looks handsome?" she whispered. Then she said to Keir, "As ready as we're going to be. It took me forever to get him to sit after he begged me to let that person inside. I hope the fear Leo feels right now humbles him a bit."

"Hmf," the boy said, eyeing Leo. "Time will tell."

Keir placed his foot behind the door and disengaged the rusted locks. Pulling the door open a slit, he looked outside.

"What do you want?" the boy said, using a harsh tone.

The door banged into the child's foot with force but he didn't budge. He moved his face away as the person outside reached his dirty hand inside and clawed the air, trying to grab him.

"Let me in!"

The boy moved with a calmness that was unnatural for someone his age. He took possession of the gun and allowed the door to swing open. Lifting the gun barrel and pressing the butt of the gun into his shoulder, he backed the man away.

"I need you need to calm down, mister," Keir said, his youth concealed in the seriousness of the moment. "I don't want to have to shoot you, but I will if you can't control yourself."

"Someone is after me and I'm desperate to get away from them," the man outside said.

Leo tried to hear every word, but the crackling and hissing coming from the fireplace interfered.

"And I don't want to be out here for another minute."

"I don't know a thing about you, mister," Keir said. "All I know is that you come banging on my door, screaming like a lunatic when I've never seen you before. Tell me why I should let you inside."

"Because I'm lost and desperate. I'm only passing through and will be out of your way once I figure out where I am and what I have to do to get out of here."

"What's your story, mister? Who is chasing you and why?"

"I don't know," the man said, panting. "They remained in the shadows, moving all around me. Thank God I found this place."

The boy took a step outside the door and swung his gaze left and right. Leo could see him relax his grip on the gun.

"Well, whoever was after you seems to be gone now," Keir said. "You can come inside, but I want you to go down the hallway on the right as soon as you get inside."

"Sure, kid, whatever you say."

"Hold it," Keir said, firming up his grip on the gun and aiming it at the man. "There are people sitting at the table inside. Don't pay them any mind, because if you do, then I'm going to either shoot you or make you leave. If I decide not to shoot you, I promise you that you won't have any chance of surviving what is out here. Do you understand that?"

"Yes."

Keir waved the gun. "Go on inside then."

"Leo?" the old woman said, and Leo looked at her. Confusion consumed him and he tried to make sense of the strange events that were unfolding around him.

"Remember what I said," the old woman said to Leo.

"What's that?"

"The man Keir just invited into the house," she said. "We need to keep the two of you separated for now."

Those words inspired Leo to look at the door again, but the man had already made it to the end of the hallway and was entering the room. Leo was able to catch a brief glimpse of a red suit. A trail of dirt outlined each shoeprint where he had stepped.

"Are they after him, too?" Leo said and looked back at the old woman.

"Yes, they are," she said.

"Why? Did we do something wrong?"

She smiled. "Something like that." She slid the mug towards him. "Why don't you drink some more of your tea while it's still warm?"

"I don't think I want any more tea." He pushed the mug away. "It makes me feel funny. I just want to know why they're after him and why we're being separated."

"The drink," she insisted and moved it towards him.

"I said that I don't want it."

"How is your shoulder? Has the pain subsided at all?"

Leo shook his head and carefully rotated his arm at the shoulder. A tinge of pain made him cringe. "No, it's hurt pretty bad. I think I might have broken it or something."

She maneuvered behind him and looked at the shoulder, humming something beautiful as she rubbed the tender area and dug her knuckles in deep.

Leo flinched.

"It's bruised but not broken."

"Pardon the interruption," Keir said from the hallway. "I trust they didn't see each other?"

The old woman stepped around the table and looked at Leo. She studied him for a moment and soon shook her head. "No, I'm certain they didn't."

"That's good." Keir smiled and set the gun down in the exact spot he picked it up from. "I'll get the other one situated." He locked the front door and disappeared down the hallway.

"Even though I've pulled that broom across the floor more times than I can count, I'm certain it's still not trained to just sweep up the dirt all on its own, now is it?" She grabbed the broom and worked slowly, sweeping the dirt into a neat pile.

"Can I ask you a question?"

She gave pause. "Your worry is back."

"My worry never left."

"It seems silly to me," she said. "I thought you might have learned that it won't change what has already happened and what is to come."

"But these things that are happening are things that I can't make sense of."

"Like what?"

"Like that guy down the hallway."

"Who, Keir?"

"No, not the boy. I want to know about the man in the suit. Why did you two work so hard to try and keep us from seeing each other?"

She leaned the broom against the wall. "I don't want to sound judgmental, Leo, but where are your manners? I've allowed you into my home and offered you comforts, and yet you ask about some guy in a suit but you still haven't asked me my name."

He felt selfish and dumb and suddenly the strange man meant nothing to him. No wonder the old woman was so scornful.

"I'm sorry, and you're right. That's rude of me and I'm embarrassed. Since I woke up in the forest, I haven't been feeling like myself. Chunks of my life are missing and everything that is happening here is so overwhelming," he said. "What has happened to me?"

"That is a great question, but you're going to need to give yourself some time. We need to start by appreciating the fire, and once we do, we can talk about you."

"I would like to know your name," he said. "And not because of what you said either. It's because I want to know. You've been very kind to me."

"My name is Twyla," she beamed, and for the first time since he arrived, she seemed to forget the discomfort of her old body and her obvious dislike of him.

"That's a nice name."

She smiled. "It means early evening, and that has always been my favorite time of night around here. But it is inevitable that the night will settle upon us, and with that comes the darkness. And when the pitch black night blankets this forest so not even the moonlight can reach the forest floor, the things outside that have been trying to get you will become restless."

"What do I have to do to get away from them?"

"Appreciate the shelter and try and focus on understanding who you were. It's important for you to know that."

Leo closed his eyes and took a deep breath.

"Appreciating this fire and your hospitality isn't that easy. What am I supposed to do when the firelight dies?"

"You can worry about that once the last log goes into those flames."

"I can't watch that fire knowing it's like sand slipping through an hourglass. It's like a countdown to something bad that I know is going to happen, and according to your words I'm helpless to stop it. But I feel I have to do something."

"By sitting here with me, you are."

"That's not good enough."

"What do you suppose is the remedy then, Leo?"

"The tea was wonderful and the heat of the fire has helped get the chill out of me, but I can't stay here. I know there must be a road or something. There has to be a way out. Maybe you would be so kind and drive me into town so I can go to the police?"

She shook her head. "I'm afraid to say that there aren't any roads here. You said it yourself that you're in the middle of nowhere."

"Then maybe you could tell me how I can reach the closet town or village?"

She tilted her head and ran a finger over the wrinkled lines on her cheek. "I haven't been out of the cabin in a long time. I'm certain there is nothing around for at least a five-day walk if you were to go out that door. But for you, it's going to be a run. And I don't think that you're going to have time to look around."

"They're going to keep chasing me, aren't they?" He looked at the bolted door and then back at her.

She nodded.

"Why is it that people show up at your door after they've been chased by those shadow things out there?"

"Maybe we should leave that alone for now because I don't think you'll like my answer."

"It can't be both ways," Leo said. "If you're saying I can't go out there then all I can do is listen, and that requires you to talk to me."

She pursed her lips and resigned with a sigh. "It's because every single person that comes here is foolish, that's why."

"So I'm a fool?"

"As foolish as the last person who came here. But the trauma you suffered came quick and you haven't given yourself time to understand what has happened."

He stared at her, his brows furrowed, and the heavy burden of all her senseless doubletalk weighed on him. He continued to search for an answer, for a hint of who he was and why he was there, but there was a void. It was big and gaping and it looked and spoke like an old woman and it refused to offer him any insight.

"I feel like you're playing with me."

"So I took you in with those things chasing after you just to toy with you, is that it?"

"I want to know what this is about."

"And you will, but these things have an order to them and you have to be patient."

"I'm not interested in your neatly wrapped ideas on how things should be. I want answers. Who are those people outside and who is that man that Keir brought into that back room?"

She shook her head. "Your order was chaos, mine is designed by experience."

"Look, I get you're lonely out here, I really do, but you trying to hang onto this secret isn't going to keep me around any longer. So why don't you tell me what you know?"

"I'm afraid that's just not possible. There is so much to who you are and what brought you here that you'd be missing out and I wouldn't be providing you with a proper service."

Leo looked at the door, but the gun was where he settled his gaze. Without thought he whirled around, grabbed the shotgun, and pulled back the hammer. The weapon was heavy in his hand and the pain in his right arm made holding it steady nearly impossible. But he wouldn't need to be accurate with a weapon like this.

"Give me my answers and tell me how to get the hell out of here or I'm going to blow your damn head off!"

"You need to calm down and think about what you're doing," Twyla said, her voice steady and calm.

"I'm not doing a damn thing you say!" he said and his body shook. "Give me some damn answers!"

"Lower the gun," Twyla said and swallowed hard. "You don't want to do this."

"You're giving me no choice. Now tell me how to get out of this god-forsaken place!" He bit his lip and aimed the gun. "Or I swear to God, I'll kill the boy after I'm done with you."

Twyla stood and Leo flinched; sparks of pain made him wince. "Watch it," he said, fighting through the pain.

"Oh, Leo, you're so broken," she said with a look of a parent that was disappointed in their child.

"Don't look at me like that!"

"I expected this from the man who went into the room with Keir, not you."

"Hey!" he said and moved the gun close to her face. "Sit your ass back down or I'll blow your brains out the back of your head. Maybe if I was to drag your body outside and let whatever is lurking around out there feed on you, it'll give me a chance to get away."

"You're a broken little boy and it breaks my heart that you are so ruined," she said.

"Shut'cher mouth!"

"Or what?"

He growled in his anger and squeezed the trigger. The hammer slammed down.

Click!

"No!" he said and reset the hammer. He squeezed the trigger again.

Click!

"It's as I said. You are broken, Leo. You're so lost and broken like so many others and that is why you're here."

4

THE STORE

The past.

Leo no longer avoided the puddles. His worn sneakers with the threadbare shoelaces were soaked through to the socks and his blue jeans clung to his legs in a cold, stiff embrace. The hoodie sagged on his head and the rainwater seeped in through the fabric and drenched his back.

A flash of lightning turned everything electric blue and a rolling rumble of thunder shook the ground beneath his feet. The hunger was deep and wrenching, remaining strong throughout his long walk through the unrelenting downpour and whipping winds, keeping his pace fast and steady.

"That thunder is making the same damn sound as you," he said, and pushed a fist into his gut to try and force it into silence. "And you haven't stopped since I left the apartment."

He approached the door of a bodega, and as he reached for the handle, the rain let up.

"It figures," he said. He had walked over two miles in a complete downpour and now that he finally decided to concede to the elements, there was a break in the weather.

As he pulled the door open, a string of bells on the backside of the door clanged against the glass, rattling loudly. He didn't see anyone at the cash register as he entered the store and he scanned the aisles as he walked across the front end. It was odd not seeing a clerk and the idea that someone had used the inclement weather to rob the store came to mind. That's something he would do if the opportunity presented itself. Maybe the clerk was tied up, beaten, or even dead in the back room.

"That's not my concern," he said, his focus firmly on satisfying his hunger.

An open, casket-style refrigerator lined with fruit printed contact paper displayed an assortment of quick meals that instantly appealed to him. Wrapped hamburgers, hot dogs, beefsteaks, tacos, and mini pizzas invited him to touch. Every one of them was tempting, but he chose a simple hamburger. It was cheaper than everything else by fifty cents and he had been running distressingly low on cash for a few days now.

You're going to need to do something about that.

He despised the voice inside his head that constantly nagged him. Ignoring it had become next to impossible and it distracted and consumed him every waking moment. Attempting to finish this task, he read and reread the simple heating instructions printed on the sticker used to hold the foil-like wrapper together before he understood them. His stomach growled so loudly that it sounded like two opposing forces were clashing inside his body. And it seemed these battles were becoming fiercer every day.

"You'll both win today, OK?" he said and bent from a sudden burst of pain as both sides clamored for dominance. "You need to stop. This isn't helping me."

Easing to a manageable level of comfort, Leo righted himself and removed the wrapper from the burger. To his surprise, the hamburger meat was well seasoned and thick and it gave off a pleasant aroma. Although the bun was soggy from trapped moisture, the price tag was at just three and a half dollars, making this an easy choice.

Placing the burger on a paper plate and into the microwave, he checked the instructions one last time and pressed the number four on the keypad beside the door. The oven came to life and the food spun around on a slow-moving carousel.

He gathered a handful of napkins and a packet of ketchup and set them down while he waited for his meal to heat. Shifting his weight from foot to foot, he looked at his pale hands and long, skinny fingers pruned by the moisture. An undeniable tremble made him shake his hands as if he could somehow dislodge whatever was wrong with him. But it never worked, so he did it again.

Cracking his knuckles, he stuffed his hands into his pockets and watched the timer counting down. This three minutes and thirty seconds felt like an eternity.

Water dropped from his hood and pitter pattered on the floor between his feet. He watched a steady drip and imagined each drop represented one of his life-altering decisions. Where did he go wrong?

"You should pick better friends," his father would tell him.

"I hate the way you talked down to me instead of to me," he said. Another water drop fell.

"You know, my father used to tell me to show him my friends and he would show me who and what I was," his mother had said to him, pushing him closer to them and further away from her.

He watched another drop fall and then another. Each one represented another criticism and another shove into a place he couldn't possibly find his way out of anymore. "You did this to me," he said and as he blocked out a memory he refused to face, another single drop fell towards the floor and splattered into a thousand tiny beads.

"How much farther until I hit bottom?" he said and shook his head.

There is no bottom. I'll always be here to help lift you up.

"I know you will," he whispered. "You've been doing that for me for so long that I can't even remember how long it has been." He thought he heard someone laughing, but he recognized it as a squeak from a door opening behind him. He looked to see a tall clerk with bad acne and big front teeth looking at him from behind boxy brown framed eyeglasses. Braces pushed his lips outwards and splotchy facial hair looked like a bad attempt at a teen trying to look like a man.

"I'm sorry," he said to Leo. "I heard you come in, but I was using the restroom."

Leo turned away. "I'm just grabbing something quick to eat and I'll be on my way." Wishing to be left alone, he watched his food twirl around.

"Are you getting the burger?" the kid said. He stepped forward and sniffed the air. "I love the way those things smell. I had one of those a little while ago. They're really good."

Leo looked over his shoulder at the boy and nodded. "Yeah, man, I'm sure they are." He didn't like the way he stood so close and the way he looked at him. He had beady eyes and there was a desperateness about him that was unsettling. Leo had no doubt that the kid was just out of high school and an outcast. Certain the boy had been on the receiving end of a few beatings from anyone that was cool. He felt he kind of deserved it. He knew him for under a minute and he already couldn't stand him.

"I haven't had a customer in hours," the clerk said. "It's not that I'm not thankful that you came in—God knows I could use the company—but I'm kind of surprised to see anyone out in this."

"Is that so?" Leo said, turning away again.

"I was listening to the radio and they said it's supposed to be like this for a few days. It's killing business."

"I could care less about some damn rainstorm. You'd be amazed what hunger can make someone do."

"Yeah, I suppose if I was hungry enough I'd come out in this, too. You lose power or something?"

Leo didn't answer.

"Stupid question I know, but I didn't. I'm Wendell," the clerk said and offered Leo his hand.

Leo laughed at his name and ignored the extended hand.

"I washed my hands before I came out of the bathroom."

"Do yourself a favor and don't stand so close to me. I don't like anyone in my space and I don't want to shake your hand."

"I'm sorry," Wendell said and backed up a step. His face turned bright red and his eyes welled with tears. He looked at Leo with a measure of distrust.

You know he's here alone, don't you?

"And I'm no one good," Leo said to Wendell, ignoring what the voice inside was implying. "And I can't offer you anything good so go and do yourself a favor and mind your own business."

The kid just stood there.

"Go," Leo said harshly and waved him away.

"OK, mister."

You need money and this is the perfect opportunity.

Wendell stared at Leo, frozen in a state of uncertainty.

"Don't look at me like that," Leo said.

Wendell looked around the store uncomfortably and Leo shook his head.

"Do you need a towel or something so you can dry off, mister?" Wendell said.

"I said to mind your own business," Leo said, his hands tightening into fists. The only solution he might have to shut this kid up would be to punch him in the mouth. He worked on picking out a spot on his face, and those big fat lips with the wire behind them were the perfect place.

"OK, sure. If you change your mind, that's cool, too."

Leo sighed and looked at Wendell from the obscurity of his hood. "What don't you understand, kid? I'm not looking to talk to you. I just want something to eat and I'll be on my way. Got it?"

He's afraid of you, and for good reason.

"Yeah, I got it," Wendell said. "I didn't mean to offend you." He walked behind the counter and sat behind the register on a rickety wooden chair that creaked underneath his weight.

"Stupid kid," Leo whispered and his attention shifted to the voice inside. It was more infuriating than the kid and he needed to tell it so. He clenched his teeth and he searched within but couldn't find it. It did that sometimes. "You need to shut up and let me do things on my own. I'm not stupid."

The microwave beeped and the smell of the prepared food calmed him. He lifted his sweatshirt and accessed his waist pack. Unzipping it, he found the money stuffed beneath items he always carried around but seldom acknowledged. Three five-dollar bills and six one-dollar bills were crumpled in a ball. Twenty-one dollars was all he had left.

You have to keep the money.

"I need to eat something. I just want to pay this kid and get out of here."

A sharp, domineering pain made him sweat and he tried to resist its show of might.

Keep twenty. That's what we're going to need to get through the night.

"But that only leaves me with a dollar to spend," he tried to reason. His words quivered along with his hands and legs.

That's not my problem.

"That's not even enough for a candy bar," he said.

You know what you have to do then.

Sweat seeped out of his pores and his heart raced.

Get me what you really need and you'll forget about your hunger.

A deep pain that rolled in the pit of his belly worked on bringing him down to his knees. But he fought back, using the fixtures to help him stand. For the moment, his desire for nourishment was strong.

"I need to eat."

What you need is me.

"You won't leave me alone until you're satisfied, will you?"

I get what I want. You should know that by now.

"Fine," Leo said and fixed his hood. He made sure it remained firmly over his head and hid his face. Walking to the counter and placing the heated burger down, he caught sight of the kid's pale pimpled face, the wire that bonded his crooked teeth, and the coke-bottle glasses that magnified his terrified eyes—making what he was going to do that much easier.

"Will that be all?" Wendell said.

"I suppose."

Wendell pressed buttons on the register.

"That'll be three dollars and seventy-three cents."

Leo dug through the waist pack and came out with a single dollar bill, ignoring the rest of the money.

What are you going to do about tomorrow?

"This is all I have," Leo said, his hand shaking.

"OK," the clerk said. "Don't worry about it. People leave change behind all the time."

He's frightened of you.

Leo looked out the glass door. It was like a ghost town outside and the streetlights showed that the unforgiving rain had started again. No one was going to come out in this.

"If you don't have the money, you can have it. It's OK."

"So what, now I'm a charity case to you all of a sudden? Do I look like a bum to you who needs your handouts?"

"No, that's not it."

"So what is it then?"

"I'm just saying that people leave behind change all the time. We can put that towards your purchase, it's no big deal, mister."

"I'm not a beggar."

The kid just looked at him.

"Two minutes ago you were trying to be my friend. Now you're trying to insult me?"

"No, it's just . . ." He blinked heavily. "I don't know what I'm supposed to say."

"How about that you're sorry."

"I'm sorry."

"No you're not. You're just a punk kid."

"I am sorry."

Leo laughed and Wendell remained silent. An obvious tremble shook his entire body.

"What are you afraid of?"

"I don't know what I did wrong to you. Whatever it is, I'm sorry, mister."

"Stop calling me mister—it's stupid." He chuckled. "You look like you're seeing the monster you've always feared and probably have the feeling that I'm about to change your night, kid."

Wendell stood and backed up a step, knocking the chair over and breaking it. "Please, just take the food and go. I don't want any trouble."

"I can't do that," Leo said. "Remember what I said about hunger and what it'll make someone do?"

Wendell whimpered. "I'm giving you what you want. Why don't you just go?"

Leo opened the waist pack and showed Wendell the grip of a pistol.

"Give me the money out of the register before I make this the worst day of your life."

Wendell just stood there, staring, frozen.

Leo withdrew the gun from the waist pack and trained it on the kid's face. "I said I want the money. Take it out of the register and do it now!"

Wendell's stare remained locked on the gun; his eyes crossed as they trained on the end of the barrel. His feet were planted firmly in place as if they had been cemented to the ground.

"Are you dumb?"

A tear fell out of Wendell's eye.

"I don't have time for this!" Leo said and reached over the counter and pounded on the register buttons. Nothing happened so he pulled on it. His hood slipped off of his head and he paused, locking eyes with the clerk. Leo hopped over the counter and punched the defenseless kid in the face. The meat-smacking thump was loud, and his glasses broke and he fell down hard. Blood dotted the floor.

Leo returned his attention to getting the money but the register didn't budge. It had been bolted to the countertop.

"Goddamn it!" Leo shouted and gave up on trying to open the register with one last mighty pull. He pressed the gun to the back of Wendell's head. "I should just kill you."

Wendell looked at Leo with eyes welled with tears and a face full of blood.

"I'd probably be doing you a favor," he said and pulled the trigger. The gun misfired. He grabbed his dollar bill and the burger and ran out of the bodega. He didn't stop running until he found an abandoned stairwell three blocks away.

Feeling safe that he wouldn't be found if the clerk called the police, he ate insatiably, whimpering at the satisfying feeling the nourishment gave him until a gut wrenching pain doubled him over and didn't let up. Adrenaline shook his limbs and he began to laugh wildly at the rush.

How could you walk out of there with nothing for me?

"I'm going to get yours right now," he said.

What about tomorrow?

"I'm worried about today," he countered and moved carefully against the possibility of more pain. Unsure if it was from the meal he just had, because he hadn't eaten in days, or if his other hunger was growing increasingly impatient, he didn't delay.

Stepping out into the rain and sticking to the shadows, he hurried on.

5

SIN

Present day.

Twyla reached out and placed a gentle hand on the weapon Leo pointed at her. She turned it away and eased it out of his loosened grip.

"Maybe I shouldn't have opened that door after all. I knew you were going to bring your trouble here and I don't like it," she said. "I should put you outside and let them deal with you. Maybe that would teach you a lesson."

"I'm . . . I'm sorry. I'm confused and desperate. This place—"

"It's not this place, Leo, it's you," she said.

Leo stared at the weapon in Twyla's hands, his jaw slack.

"Why do you have such a surprised look on your face?"

"The gun," Leo said. "Why was it unloaded?"

"Because it doesn't need to be loaded." She leaned towards him and raised a brow. "Look at what you tried to do, and you wonder why it's unloaded?"

"But what about the things outside?"

"What about them, Leo? What do you have against them?"

"They were chasing me! If you don't have ammunition in the gun then how do you expect to fend them off?"

Twyla set the gun down next to the door. "What gave you the impression I wanted to fend them off?"

"Because there's something wicked about them. Can't you sense it?"

"I suppose," she said, and walked to the table and sat. "But it's not directed towards me."

"These things, not people, are living in the forest that surrounds your home and you're not worried about that?"

She shook her head. "Not in the least. I'm just an old woman that's been crippled by time. What do you think they'd want with me?"

"I don't know what their motives are. What about Keir?"

"What about him?"

"Don't you fear for him?" Leo said and moved close enough to Twyla to smell her bad breath. "I think those things are the real monsters that hide underneath his bed and you don't do anything to help protect him from them?"

"You misunderstand them, Leo," she said with a smile. "They envy him. Long for his innocence." She rubbed her face and thought for a moment. "I suppose I do, too. He's so full of life and his company is refreshing. I'm surprised his time here hasn't changed him, taken from his innocence. But he reminds me of what I once had and let go. I wasted so much time by holding onto empty wishes and chasing after desires for a better tomorrow and never focused on what I had that day."

Leo watched Twyla's anger transform into a somber expression of remorse.

"I was young and full of life like he is, but that was a long time ago." She sighed and looked around. "Now instead of wishing for tomorrow, I wonder if there will be one. I try and imagine what it must be like to know a body without pain and a mind without such worry."

"The boy," Leo said. "Who is he to you?"

"He's just a child that's here for people like you."

"For people like me?" The skin on Leo's forehead wrinkled as he grasped for the meaning behind her words. "What's that supposed to mean?"

"Look, you're going to have to do some of the thinking for yourself." She looked around the room, her face twisting back into its normal mold of irritation. "I'm a tired old woman and your questions are wearing on me. Stop standing so close to me, looking so dumb."

Leo clenched his teeth, biting back his anger. She had no defenses against him and her words were pointed and provoking. He figured she must have something in that dark room that was watching them so he backed away, hoping to find some meaning to all of this.

"Maybe I shouldn't be so tough on you," she whispered and let out a deep breath. "Sometimes I feel like I've been living in this valley forever, confined to this cabin, waiting on people who will never appreciate my work."

"I appreciate it."

"You?" She laughed. "You have a strange way of showing people your appreciation. If you've already forgotten, you pointed a gun in my face, pulled the trigger, and have defied my every word since you arrived."

Shame moved his gaze elsewhere. "That was an error in judgment," he said, his tone barely above a whisper. "Desperation can make you do the dumbest things. And I get why the gun is unloaded."

She eyed him with firm indifference. "Ah." Her lips curled in and she watched the fire. "You think you know, but you don't. And you don't have to pretend to be kind or thoughtful because you're not."

"Why would you say that about me?"

"Because I know who you are."

"The gun is unloaded because the people who get lost in these woods become desperate and they might turn the weapon on you. I get it."

"That was always a concern, but no one has gone as far as you. And there have been a lot of people to come and go from here."

It was true. He had a clear understanding of the difference between right and wrong but rarely paid it attention. It was as if he had shoved it aside and it had remained there ever since, just out of reach. "I don't know why I did that."

"Oh, please, Leo, don't kid yourself. You're not sorry." She stared at him, challenging him. "And you know why you did it, but you have a way of tucking things away so you don't have to face them. You do that because you're a coward."

She retrieved the gun and placed it on the table. It hit the wood with a thud and sounded heavy.

"It is used to ensure compliance from the people," Twyla said. "It is merely a prop. Everyone who comes here is frightened and looking for refuge. They've been chased through an unfamiliar forest with hardly any light or time for thought."

"They're wicked," Leo said.

"What do you expect them to be after what they've been through?"

"How am I supposed to know? I don't know what they've been through."

"You might not remember, but they do, and it is nothing good."

She picked up the gun and pointed it at Leo, centering it on his chest.

"It's vital we gain control over the people immediately. We've got to get them refocused and the shotgun is instantly recognizable to most anyone, no matter the trauma they've been through, and it sobers them quickly."

She lifted the gun, holding it mere inches from his face, keeping it steady between his eyes. Her finger hugged the trigger.

He stared down the barrel of the gun and even though it wasn't loaded, it still made him nervous. He remembered when he first faced the weapon how it had held him between his fear of being shot and what was chasing him. He didn't stand a chance against a slug that could easily have punched a hole through his face.

She lowered the gun. "And the things you were running from serve a greater purpose than your fear. But you can't see past that."

"What purpose do they serve?"

She tittered. "Yes, Leo, what purpose indeed?"

He stared at her.

"Think," she said and tapped her temple with a crooked finger.

He shook his head; her old crippled body made him uncomfortable. "What is there to think about? They scratch your walls and taunt me. All I want to do is get away from them but they won't leave me be!"

"No, they won't. Knowing that, when you get back outside, you need to run like you did. That's all you can do. Run until you can't run anymore."

He whimpered.

"Here, put this back for me," Twyla said and handed Leo the shotgun. He took it and walked to the door.

"I know you're scared, Leo, I can hear it in your voice, see it in your eyes. It's tangible and I don't like it either, but this—" she swirled her finger in a circle—"this here is your burden. And I know you don't think so, but I'm doing all I can for you. But you're stubborn."

He set the gun down. "I'm not! I'm frustrated because there has to be something more than you're telling me," he said. "This doesn't make sense."

"What doesn't make sense?"

"None of it! You, the boy, and that man in there with him. The forest and this cabin and that black room in the back." He licked his lips, his wide eyes unblinking.

"You may not be able to see it, but it all makes perfect sense."

"No, none of it makes sense," he said, shaking his head. "I want to know about the things outside. I've been asking about them since I got here and I still don't know a thing about them."

"They gather over time and they wait. Some develop and others do not. It depends on choices that are made. They howl in the woods for a long time . . . their physical and emotional suffering is deep. It's a primal scream of pain, and when you hear it, you can't help but feel bad and be afraid. Over time they learn to focus that pain and turn it into rage and prepare for the hunt they know is coming. It is a natural instinct they possess."

"Why are they here?"

She stared at the door.

"And why do they hunt people?"

"Because that is what they do. It is their function. I've already told you that."

In a sudden spark of rage, Leo thrust himself forward and pounded the tabletop. The book bounced and the glass of tea spilled over and dumped its contents before it rolled onto the floor and shattered. "Stop giving me half answers!"

Twyla looked at the broken glass scattered across the floor. The book was wet from the spill. "You see? You don't appreciate anything!"

"You're toying with me!"

"I'm not toying with you, Leo! I've been trying to educate you. And you should try and show me and my home some respect by controlling yourself. You and this rage you have. What is it all about?"

Twyla picked up the book and stood. She turned the pages and Leo could see black ink spread across the leaves. He thought he saw sketches, but the pages flipped too fast and the lighting in the room was murky at best.

"Perhaps this outburst was another error in judgment?" Twyla said.

"No!" Leo said, and he tore the book out of her hands. Tea dripped off of the spine. "I meant it and would do it again if it would get you to talk plainly instead of in circles."

"You are a fool!" Twyla said. "Give me back the book!"

"This is important to you, isn't it?" He walked to the fireplace and held the binding above the flames. The fiery tendrils touched the old parchment, blackening the edges. "Tell me about this valley I'm in or I swear I'll drop it in the fire!"

"You are broken and sinful, Leo, and your chance to improve passed a long time ago."

"And you are a lonely old lady who's miserable." He lowered the book and the edge of the pages caught fire, spewing soot up the chimney.

"OK," she said, and at the sight of the flame-bitten book she became frail. "Don't burn that. I'll tell you what you want to know."

He snuffed the flames. "What is this place?"

"There are numerous cabins in the valley and they all have someone young and old in them. Every day they wait for someone to come. These people who come are much like yourself. Everyone has a story to tell, but they all end up the same."

Leo was filled with a sudden sense of hope. He set the book down on the table and the pages smoldered. Twyla patted the cinder away and took the book, holding it tightly against her chest.

"These other cabins, I could go to them," he said. "And maybe they'd be able to help me. They might have a car or a telephone or know of a road or have defenses against the people in the wild."

She shook her head. "These cabins and the keepers are here to assist those who are lost and are in need of shelter. Our resources are limited and our purpose is only to help people to remember."

"Remember what?"

"The past and their lives. What do you remember about yours?"

"Nothing before the chase." A profound hush lingered. "I hit my head hard."

"That has nothing to do with why you can't remember."

He felt the lump on his head. It was big and sensitive. He didn't need to debate what he knew to be truth. "Maybe one of them knows a way out of the valley?"

"I don't think you understand, Leo. There is nowhere for you to go and yet you continue to focus on things that are unchangeable."

"There has to be a way."

"No, there isn't." She inspected the book. "There is much about the valley you don't understand. It is impossible for you to find the other cabins and to find your way out of these woods."

"But if I found this place then that means I can find the others, too."

"No, you can't," she said, and placed the book down. "I can hear your hope and understand your desperation, but you need to listen to the things I'm telling you."

He toiled, unwilling to let go of his hope.

"These other places are tucked away in the forest, hidden deep, never to be found," she said. "The only way to discover one is to be channeled through intricate paths by the things outside. They bring you where you need to be so you can understand."

His hope crumbled into a pile of weariness and his shoulders fell at the disappointment of her words. "What do they want me to understand?"

"Their plight," she said. "They want you to know their plight."

The fire crackled and the logs that crisscrossed collapsed, sending embers up the chimney. Although brief, the burst of heat that belched from the fireplace was intense. The pile of ash beneath the wood was an indication of how much time he'd spent inside the cabin already.

"Go ahead and place three more logs into the fireplace," she said. "The last thing you want is the room to go dark."

Leo took three logs out of the oval rack and placed them in the center of the flames. Within moments, they were engulfed with orange, yellow, and blue, cracking and hissing as they reached a boil.

"There are only six logs left," he said.

"I need to remind you that when the wood has burned away, your stay here will come to an end. The comforts of my home will no longer be yours to use."

He stared into the flames, deep in thought. "The man you have hiding in the back. I know he was brought here so we can confront each other about something. Why else would you have worked so hard to hide us from each other?"

She looked at him with a calm that revealed nothing.

"Use your time wisely, Leo. Your confusion is deep and your refusal to listen to what I'm telling you is putting you at a terrible disadvantage."

He clenched his fists. "I want you to stop avoiding my questions and tell me who the man is and what he has to do with me."

She hobbled to him, stepping over the broken glass. "He has everything to do with you." She took him by the arm. "But you can't expect to understand who he is if you don't know yourself. I am going to help you remember but you need to be patient. Maybe you should wash up. I'll bring you your clothes and you can dress once you've bathed. That'll give you a chance to relax."

Leo sat without further protest and monitored Twyla as she shuffled into the dark room. He hated that part of the cabin. It gave him the feeling of dread. His hands trembled and he interlocked his fingers to keep them from shaking. But the more he tried to resist it, the more powerful it became. His heart slammed in his chest and he broke out in a sweat. He dropped the blanket and felt the need to flee intensify. Standing in his underwear, he looked at the door and was certain he could outrun them—but he needed his clothes.

"Here, this should help you relax," Twyla said and stepped out of the room that concealed everything. Pushing a small cart that had a bowl, pitcher, and rag on its top, she struggled to set the wooden bowl on the tabletop.

"Come," she said and handed him the rag. She hummed a tune and poured steaming hot water into the hand basin. She set his folded clothes down in a neat pile on the table.

"What's happened to me?" he said.

"Let's wash away all of the dirt you collected running away from them outside," she said and set a bar of soap down. Picking up the rag, she dipped it in the water and rang it out. With a gentle hand, she worked slowly to clean his face. "I wish there was something I could say or do to help you with your worry, but I can't. Your frustration is only going to make things worse for you."

He watched her dip the rag into the water, withdraw it, and ring it out again. The water turned brown. She reached to continue cleaning him, but he pulled away.

"Stop it!"

"What is it?"

He dressed quickly.

"You, this place, and whatever is happening to me. I've got to get out of here!"

"I should clean that wound on your stomach. I don't think you realize how bad it is."

"No, it's fine," he said and didn't hesitate. He walked to the door, disengaged the barrel bolts, yanked the handle, and like Twyla had warned, was greeted with a darkness so deep it put a crack in his resolve and made him waver.

"You shouldn't do that," she said.

Her warning encouraged him to defy his trepidation. He wasn't going to get the answers he was seeking and the only way to escape this madness was to try and get to another cabin.

"Leo," she said. "Think about what you're doing. They won't let you get past the tree line."

He despised her warnings and for a moment was able to see past his fears and face things for how they were. Twyla had been manipulating him since he arrived and there was no question she was trying to keep him inside the cabin. Maybe it had something to do with that man inside the other room with that kid or maybe she was just crazy. But that didn't matter anymore because the answers weren't here.

"Goodbye, Twyla," he said and faced the darkness with determination.

"I'm watching prey step into the mouth of a lion," she said. "You're not ready to confront what is out there."

"Like hell I ain't," he said. "What I'm not ready to face is another moment of your doubletalk and your attempts at distracting me and keeping me worried. I'm willing to take my chances out there."

"You think you're being brave but you're being irrational. Life has lessons and some come at a steep price. You're not ready to do that."

Ignoring her words, he exited the cabin, took five steps out the door, and stopped. The trees that circumvented the small cabin came alive and they swayed from a strong, swooping gust of wind. A loud snap off to his left turned his attention and a large tree fell over. The leafy end shook as it crashed to the ground almost as if it had waved farewell to him. Then something off to his right caught his attention. Whatever it was, it was big and it moved fast. Parting the foliage as it ran on two feet, it squatted down once it cleared the greenery. It used its hands to propel itself forward with great speed and strong, bountiful leaps.

"Oh my God!" Leo said and turned to run into the cabin. He stumbled but managed to right himself. When he entered the cabin, he tried to push the door closed but the brute that chased him hit the door with explosive power and knocked Leo over. Sliding across the floor, he stopped inches away from the dark room, the cold air seeping out of it like dead fingers caressing his skin.

The beast stood upright, beat its chest, and roared. Driving its fists onto the floor with a thump next to Leo's head, it went nose to nose with him, staring with untamed eyes he didn't dare meet. What hovered above him was something out of his worst nightmare, and it was alive.

"Twyla, help me, please," Leo said and pressed his body flat.

"I've been trying to do that but you wanted to leave."

He clamped his eyes shut and turned his head away. The heat of the monster's breath drummed off the side of his face and the foul odor nauseated him.

"I see a fool," Twyla said. "One that will never learn."

He held his breath and clamped his eyes shut.

"Hamartia, leave him be," Twyla said. "He's pitiful."

The crazed fiend continued to huff. Gobs of drool spilled out of its mouth and fell onto Leo's cheek and oozed onto the floor.

"You are not his," Twyla shouted. "I said to leave him be!"

The beast sniffed him, the wet nose cold.

"Hamartia, I said to come here now!" Twyla said as if she were commanding an animal.

"You're not fast enough," the thing whispered in a muffled voice he was sure was female. It turned away and left Leo.

Slowly and unsure if it was safe to move, Leo eased himself into a sitting position. Spying the black beyond the open door he could see the fallen tree and forestry hugged in night.

The beast was nowhere in sight.

He hurried across the floor in a crawl and pushed the door closed and it banged shut. Pressing his back against the wall, he ran a shaking hand through his hair and shrank as he tried to understand what that thing was.

"You allowed it inside," Twyla said, pulling Leo out of his thoughts. "I don't want you to worry. It can't harm you."

Her words gave Leo the chills and he hopped to his feet. Eyes wide and limbs shaking, he emerged from his tunnel vision and saw that the beast was next to Twyla, staring back at him. Lumps knotted the head and the face was twisted. Clumps of hair were missing and strands that remained were long and unkempt, entangled with filth. The untamed eyes locked on him and they were crammed with a hate so tangible, Leo desperately needed to escape it.

"God, please help me!" he said and ran for the door. When he pulled the door open, he was faced with countless malformed things. They varied in age and they moaned and reached for him, moving forward in a slow, disorganized manner.

"You!" a single voice from the crowd yelled and everything—even Leo's heart—went still. The middle aged thing hobbled forward, naked and deformed like all the rest, and the crowd parted for it.

"Me?" Leo said and could feel Hamartia's presence behind him, keeping him at the door. With nowhere left to go, he whimpered. "What do you want from me?"

"Revenge."

"I get him first," another from the crowd said, and Leo spotted him right away. His deformation went into his limbs and he was forced to pull himself across the ground, dragging limp legs behind him.

"Please, I don't know what I did to you," Leo said and watched as they approached him, paralyzed by his inability to escape what was coming for him and what stood behind.

The male thing that crawled on the ground pulled at the other one, trying to get ahead of him. But the first one that called out was stronger and had the use of his legs. He managed to outpace the other, drawing near Leo and stopping at the threshold of the cabin.

"We are no longer yours," the deformed thing mumbled, his voice muted by swollen lips and crooked, rotted teeth in a misaligned jaw. "You are ours!" He hit Leo in the chest with a fist that had no fingers and Leo fell to the floor and gasped for air.

The crowd outside roared with a cheer. To Leo it sounded muffled, as if he'd been pulled beneath the surface of some surreal new reality.

"Try and relax and concentrate on catching your breath," Twyla said, standing over him.

A bottomless void made up of carnage and misunderstanding threatened to consume him and the only thing he could do was concentrate on her voice.

"Oh, Leo, what did you do?"

The door banged shut and reality slammed back into his head. Confused and desperate to escape the things that wished to do him harm, he got to his feet and staggered down the hallway and tried Keir's door.

"Help me," he tried to say, but only managed a dull wheeze. The door was locked.

"Get a hold of yourself, Leo," Twyla said.

He leaned against the wall and gasped, his lungs on fire.

"Leo?" Twyla said. She was back at the table with Hamartia. "The others are locked outside and if she was one of yours, she wouldn't have let you go on my command. Now come and sit. You have nothing to be afraid of when it comes to this one."

"I don't like it," Leo said.

"When a child is born with a defect, is it the child's fault?" Twyla said.

"No, of course not."

"Then Hamartia deserves love. Doesn't she?"

Leo stepped out of the hallway and the predator watched him. As if propelled by a natural rage, Hamartia charged and pinned him against the wall. Growling and sniffing him frantically, she whispered in his ear, "Soon it will be your time to run."

She let him go and walked to the logs, grabbed a stack, and threw them on the fire.

"Soon," she said and sat next to Twyla.

"The wood!" Leo said but didn't dare move.

"It must be burned anyways. Hamartia's outbursts are normal considering what she's been through. She can't harm you though and she's only doing what she knows," Twyla said and stroked the head of the monster. "The sooner you go, the sooner she gets her turn. Do you understand?"

"No."

Bang.

The door rattled and Leo flinched.

A cold, sinister voice seeped through the door and said, "Leopold."

He looked at the door. "What the hell do you want from me?" he shouted.

Twyla answered. "Your fretting has stirred the ones that want you. I told you to calm yourself because you're only going to make it worse. Ignore what it is saying. They're going to try and unnerve you." She tapped her temple. "Try and get inside your head."

"Come, sinful one, get what is coming to you," the voice under the door said, hissing. "Open the door and let me inside."

6

THE TRANSACTION

The past.

The torrential downpour continued with no signs of stopping. Water swelled through street gutters and spilled into storm drains like a fast moving river that jumped off the side of a cliff. Lightning flashed and the sky grumbled in anger.

Saturated to the skin, Leo galloped across the unoccupied road and hurried under a rusted awning. He was winded and needed to rest. Wiping his face with his hands and trying to see inside the dark store, the only thing that was visible was a partially dressed mannequin donning dry clothes and an expression that seemed to say he was more worthy of the clothes than Leo.

Wrapping his fingers around a security gate, he shook it and it rattled loudly.

Stop acting so foolish.

"I don't like the way that thing is looking at me."

It's plastic.

The cheap burger he stole from the bodega hurt his stomach and a deep chill made him shake.

"I'd love something dry to put on and it's mocking me."

Shut up and move it.

Looking down the empty street, it seemed everyone but him had stayed indoors.

Go on, I said. Standing here isn't going to get me what I need.

Compelled to carry on, he stuck to the shadows, pausing here and there to avoid detection from the police. Although he didn't see any, he was sure they were out. They had begun to patrol the neighborhood in an attempt to clean it up. Saint Nick had turned the area into a hotbed of violence that stopped at nothing to instill fear and compliance in the community. It was a classic game of cat and mouse.

"I'm doing the people of this neighborhood a service," Leo heard Saint Nick say one day. "I've given them jobs and something to do. That's saying a lot—especially in this economy."

To Leo, there was a measure of truth to that. His savvy business acumen and his ability to go from street thug to a kingpin was something to admire. His wit often went untamed, as did his violent nature, and he always seemed to be steps ahead of the police. He managed to do that by paying his people well and by constantly adjusting the process his clients had to go through in order to get their next high.

"Second window on the right," he recalled, his legs weak. "Take it easy, I'm almost there."

Though most of Leo's memories had giant holes in them, he never had any trouble remembering Saint Nick's instructions, no matter how complicated they were. Looking left and then right before he slipped down a dark alleyway, he hurried to the second window on the right. The glass pane was covered by a heavy curtain that revealed nothing about the inside of the dwelling. He tapped the metal frame with his fingernails with a specific beat, counted to ten, and repeated the process two more times.

As Leo rocked from foot to foot the downpour persisted and the response felt like it would never come.

Knock again!

He wrestled with the idea of doing that but shook his head and tried to reason with his worry. Yesterday, or maybe it was the day before, he was here, and if things had changed they would have told him.

How would they let you know? You don't own a phone and you sleep in a basement you found.

He had been warned not to repeat the secret knock unless he was compromised.

"No," he whispered feeling as though he was in the fight of his life.

They're ignoring you. I said knock again!

"No."

Do it!

Submitting to the voice inside, he motioned to knock again but a sudden sharp and excruciating flash of pain bent him over and he felt his insides squeeze like hands were twisting his stomach. He vomited hard, straining against the forceful spasms. Thick and carrying a strong odor, he watched the rainwater work on washing away the partially digested meat and bread.

"Please answer," he whispered and didn't bother to wipe his mouth. Instead, he pushed his fist into his belly and it helped to lessen the ache. Then, a responding tap let him know they were there and he stood, trying to hide his distress.

"Thank God," he said, and the curtain moved aside. A bright beam of light from a flashlight shined in his face and he clamped his eyes shut. Unzipping his waist pack, he withdrew the crumpled up money and held it out for them to see. The light blinked off.

"Were you followed?" the muffled voice from behind the glass said.

"No. I was careful."

"Go around and put your money in the hole," the voice said, and the curtain closed.

He walked around the back side of the brick building, stopped at a window well, and knelt in a puddle. Squeezing his fist around the money, he noticed his knuckles were swollen. He must have punched the nerdy clerk with the pinky and ring finger knuckles. The top of his hand had already begun to turn black and blue but there was no pain. At least nothing could compare to what already ailed him.

Moving his clenched fist through the hole where a missing pane of glass served as the exchange point, his hand shook. The anticipation of being relieved of the physical and emotional burden of his addiction was a finish line he went to great lengths every day to cross. And in this moment he began to weep because it was finally about to happen.

"Thank you," he said, his heart racing and his emotions on fire, beating back the chill. "I need this so bad and have felt terrible today."

Leo was torn from his bliss as a powerful hand latched onto his wrist and yanked him forward. His face smashed into the side of the brick building and he saw stars and blood filled his mouth. The immense strain on his shoulder and the throb in his face made him wince and his thoughts became confused.

"What are you doing?" he whimpered, unsure what was happening to him, the pressure like nothing he had ever felt before.

"Saint Nick wants a word with you, Leo."

In his struggle against the thing inside and in his desperation to satisfy it, Leo had forgotten about his debt to his dealer.

"Leopold Conroy," Saint Nick said from within the basement. He was standing close and was probably looking up at Leo's exposed gut, the fancy stainless steel knife with the ivory handle he always carried no doubt at the ready. "Have you come to pay me what you owe?"

"I can't," Leo said, his fear so intense he forgot about his pain.

"You can't?"

"No, it's not that. I forgot." He spat blood.

"How can you claim to forget such a thing?"

He wanted to scream but spoke through clenched teeth instead. "The past few days have been a blur." The pressure from being pulled against the house made it hard for him to breathe. "I tried to get some money from a store but I wasn't able to get anything."

"Only a junkie would come here and tell me they've forgotten about my money and some ridiculous story about some store."

"It's the truth," Leo said, his teeth scraping against the brick. "That's how I busted up my hand."

They twisted his hand around and he thought they were probably inspecting it.

"Do you take me for a fool, Leo?"

"No," he said and tried to shake his head but couldn't.

"If your story is true then you did it to cover your next high, not to pay me back. That's how you do things. You don't think I know that about you?"

"I do, but it's hard for me to think that far ahead sometimes."

"So, why are you here?"

"Because it won't leave me alone."

"And how do you presume to think that's somehow my problem, Leo?"

"Because you have it and it's all I can think about."

"You should've come with something more than a few crumpled up bills. I find it insulting. You need to go back out and get me my money while it's still fresh on your mind."

"I don't think I can. It has me good today and I need something to shut it up."

"I can't help you if you're not willing to help yourself."

"Please, I have enough money for what I need now. Just get me past this so I can work on getting you your money."

"Are you hearing me, Leo?"

The strain on his arm increased and tendons in his wrist and shoulder felt like they were going to break.

"Why should I give you anything?"

"Because you're Saint Nick and you're generous and understanding," Leo said. "But I don't want handouts. I will pay you for it."

Someone down there laughed.

"Nicely said, Leo, and yes, you're going to pay one way or the other," Saint Nick said.

"But what happened wasn't my fault."

"Oh, it was."

"How so?"

"You're responsible for the inventory you're given, Leo. How do I know you didn't sell it and make up some story so you didn't have to pay me? Isn't that how a desperate mind works?"

The image of the body etched into his floor came crashing back into his mind and he reached for the fear and physical pain instead. It was easier to deal with than trying to face that.

"How could you say that?" Leo said.

"Because you're an addict, Leo, and I don't trust you. It's not personal . . . it's a business decision. And doing business has a price."

Leo felt a forceful tug on his jacket and his belly stung. It itched something fierce but he couldn't scratch it because his arm was outstretched.

"I'm going to pay you back," he said. "Every dime of it, I swear. I just need more time."

"I've given you more than a month because I felt bad for you."

"Please," Leo said.

"You've reached the deadline I set and now I'm supposed to turn away and believe you're going to pay me my money somehow? Do you want people to think I'm weak?"

"I beg you. No one is here and they'll never know. I've got nowhere to go and you're the only one who can get me through this. What I see when I close my eyes is haunting and I haven't been able to focus."

"And you think your putting this shit in your body is going to help you focus?"

Leo grunted. "Please, ease up," he said. The wall he was being pressed against was rough and scraped away his cold, wet skin.

"Maybe you'd be willing to give a finger as payment?" Saint Nick said, and whoever held Leo pried his fingers open. "Perhaps it can be a message to others?"

"No," Leo said and tried pulling away. But they held him in place. "Please, man, don't do this. You've known me for a long time, allowed me to work for you. You know I'm good for it."

"If you were good for it, you would have brought me my money tonight."

"Dammit, please listen to me! Give me a fix tonight and I'll give you double the money tomorrow night."

"And where do you think you're going to get the money from?"

"My father."

"He won't give it to you."

"Then I'll take it from him by force if I have to."

Leo could hear them talking in hushed voices but the pitter-patter of rain interfered with his being able to hear what was being said. The pull on his arm eased, but only a little.

"I'm not in the business of looking the other way," Saint Nick said. "That doesn't make good business sense, does it?"

"No, it doesn't."

"It has you bad, you know that? You've become reckless."

"I know," he said and planted his free hand on the wall next to his face to try and take some of the pressure off of his cheek and neck. His shoulder popped and his fingers went numb. He could still taste blood and his lips were puffy. "I think you knocked out my teeth."

"Let him go," Saint Nick said, and whoever held him let go. Leo fell over and flopped in a puddle. Looking at his swollen hand—that still had all of its fingers—panic came when he noticed the money was gone and there weren't any drugs.

Get up, Leo, and get what you need.

"I can't," he said, and began to weep. "They'll kill me."

No they won't. They want to be paid.

Struggling to his knees, his sorrow turned to desperation.

Go out swinging if you must.

He scowled and looked at the window. One good kick and he could be inside. With his good hand he reached down and felt the weight of the gun in the waist pack.

"You're a mess, Leo," someone behind him said. "Do you think I like seeing you like this?"

Leo flinched and turned to see Saint Nick looking down at him, his arms folded across his chest. One of his lackeys stood behind him and held a big umbrella, keeping his boss out of the rain. Dressed in a bright red three-piece suit with red shoes, the scent of Saint Nick's cologne overpowered the filthy alleyway. Two armed men stood on either side of him and everything about them quelled Leo's idea to fight.

"What were you reaching for?"

"Nothing," Leo said.

"You're angry and I don't want you to direct that towards me," Saint Nick said. "I've been kind to you. I've given you opportunities." He stepped towards Leo and his henchmen followed, staying close. "I've given you gifts and have allowed you to escape the demons you run from. But you've stolen from me, mistaken my kindness as a weakness."

"I didn't steal from you. I swear it."

"Then where is my stuff?"

"I don't know."

"How about my money?" Saint Nick said. "Where is that?"

"I don't know. Someone stole it."

"I don't think I believe that. What I don't understand about you is why you didn't take advantage of the opportunities your father gave you."

"I didn't want that."

"You were handed a silver spoon, Leo!" Saint Nick stared, his anger tangible. "You're disorganized and tragic, not a businessman. You weren't forced to do this like I was. You chose it and failed miserably. You've gotten yourself hooked on it."

"I wanted to be my own man."

Saint Nick bent down and grabbed Leo's chin with a gloved hand. He looked into his eyes; the man's power made him shrivel. "So tell me, now that you're your own man, do you like what you've become?"

"No," Leo said with shame, but he couldn't remember being anything else.

"I told you not to touch the stuff, but you didn't listen." He slapped Leo's face. "You walked away from something good and chose the streets. You chose the shit instead of the gold and you want people to feel bad for you."

Saint Nick stood and took a step back, snapping his fingers. In response, one of the men stripped the waist pack off of Leo and handed it to Saint Nick. He looked through the pack and held up the gun.

"You've brought a weapon to my place of business?"

"It's not meant for you."

"Then for who?"

"Whoever has enough money."

"Spoken like a true junkie." Saint Nick handed the waist pack to one of his men, turned to Leo, and unsheathed the ivory-handled knife. The blade gleamed in the dim light of the alleyway and he held it close to Leo's face. "Maybe I should put my initials in your cheek so you remember this moment for the rest of your life."

"No, please, I'll make this right."

"I'm satisfied for now because I've already left my mark, Leo," Saint Nick said and moved the knife down by Leo's gut. "Look." He showed him the slice in his clothing and flesh. "You are so out of it you don't even feel your body being cut."

"It was because of the pressure on my face and shoulder."

"Whatever you say. Let that be a reminder that I'm no longer playing with you. You have until tomorrow night to bring me my money. If you don't, I'm going to use the gun in that bag of yours to kill you."

Leo stared at the cut and Saint Nick dropped a baggie into Leo's lap.

"That's enough to get you through the night."

"Thank you," Leo said and took the baggie. He handled it as if it were a precious gem. Struggling to his feet, he dared not look at Saint Nick as he exited the alleyway.

When he reached the sidewalk, the injuries he suffered to his face, arm, and stomach became prevalent. He leaned against a telephone pole and suffered in silence.

Leo noticed a sign in the window of a small store adjacent the drug building that was separated by the alleyway he had just emerged from. It was illuminated by the flickering streetlamp. The sign read:

Take a break from your pain and the cold.
God knows your suffering.
Are you hungry?
Lost?
Come break bread.
Hot meals served 4am to 6pm every day.

7

THE BOY AND HIS TOY

Present day.

The man in the three-piece suit, red in color, rested his head against the wall and breathed heavily. He began to giggle but it soon turned into a fitful laugh that doubled him over and hurt his stomach.

"What's so funny, mister?" Keir said as he entered the room and pushed the wooden door closed. It shut with a heavy thud.

"I outran them all!" He gasped. "There had to be twenty of them, maybe more!"

"Who did you outrun, mister?"

"I don't know who they are, but they were fast. But I was faster and managed to stay ahead of them and find my way to safety."

"That you did, mister. At least for now."

The man in the red suit rested his back against the wall and continued to giggle as he thought about how close he was to being caught and how he managed to escape. "They almost got me for a minute there because I didn't think you were going to open the door." His laughter faded and his smile dimmed. "Why did it take you so long to come and let me inside?"

"I didn't know you were out there, mister."

"How could you not hear me? I was screaming for you to open the door."

"I was in this room here and it is hard to hear anything that goes on out there. But I came once I knew you were out there."

"Well, that's a good thing because I was about to kick the door down," the man said, his face covered with sweat. He wiped it away with the back of his hand and examined himself. With the exception of the filth on his shoes, he had managed to keep himself relatively clean. Brushing away leaves and twigs that snagged his custom-made jacket and pants, he sighed. "Look at what they did to my suit."

"There's no one here that cares about the way you dress or how you look."

"I can see that. A boy dressed as a girl?" He smiled. "Peculiar, don't you think?"

"It is inspired from a generation much better than yours," Keir said and stepped past the man. He walked to the center of the room and stood with his hands clasped. "You could learn some things from the way people used to live. They had manners and were thankful for the things they had."

"Screw this," the man said and reached for the door handle.

"Unlike you, mister."

Distracted, he looked at Keir.

"Yeah, OK, anyways, where am I?" the man said.

"You're in my room, mister."

Bizarre sketches of dark faces hung on the walls. The man thought he saw glimpses of things that looked similar to those he saw as he ran, but everything had happened so fast he couldn't be sure.

"What's with the pictures, kid?"

Keir watched the man for a second before answering him. "They're acknowledgments."

"Of what?"

Keir turned away and walked into a darkened corner. Kneeling in front of an old wooden chest, he lifted the heavy cover and the hinges squealed. Rubbing his face as searched the innards inside the box, he rested his elbows on the thick rim and contemplated something.

"Are you going to answer me, kid?"

"Now where did I put that?" the boy said, ignoring the man. He began a careful search through the contents of the box, picking at things.

"Hey, kid, what are you deaf or something?"

"I hear you, mister. I'm just looking for something for us to play with."

"Do I look like I want to play games with you, kid?"

"No, but you should. Now, let me see if I can find it."

Keir continued his search.

The man approached him, closing the lid on Keir. "Let's start off by you giving me something I can wipe my shoes off with."

"I don't have anything for that," Keir said and lifted the lid again, resuming his search.

"I got mud all over my shoes and it looks like I stepped in shit."

Keir looked at the man, his face scrunching into a look of disapproval. "Don't you use profanity around me, mister."

"Sure, kid," the man said. "Are you the son of that preacher man?"

"I'm not sure what you're talking about, mister."

"The one who opened up that food pantry on my street corner?"

Keir shook his head.

"I thought you were a lot taller and a bit older though."

"I think you have me confused with someone else, mister."

"Before I got to the forest, I remember some kid running away from me in an alleyway."

"It wasn't me."

"Either way, I don't care about the church being there. That's a good thing for the community. It adds some good. But tell the pastor not to interfere in my business, OK?"

"Sure, mister, whatever you say," Keir said and drummed his fingers on the lip of wood. "I don't understand . . . I was just using them last night."

The man looked at the defenseless child. The thought of striking him flashed through his mind but he restrained. "Did you hear what I said to you?"

"Yeah, I heard you, mister, but you're not hearing me."

"You're a smartass, do you know that?"

Keir slapped the box, stood, and pointed at the man. "I'm not kidding, mister. I asked you not to use profanity around me."

The man raised his hands. "Sure, kid, whatever."

Keir busied himself by moving things around inside the chest, but this time with a bit more determination.

"So, what is it with you, kid? Does your daddy being a preacher have something to do with the reason why you're so serious?"

"He ain't my daddy and I just don't like vulgar language, that's all. I wish people would understand how things that come out of their mouths make them sound so foolish."

"You're trying to convince me you're not the son of the preacher and yet you're preaching to me?"

"I'm going to tell you the truth, mister."

"Well if you want the truth, I think you're too damn serious for a kid your age," the man said. "Shit. Fuck. What's the big deal, kid? They're just words."

Keir's face reddened. "The things you say—"

"Yeah, yeah. Do this and don't do that, I get it. He should let you be a kid so you don't grow up hating him. All of his pissing and moaning is only going to make you defy him."

The man pressed his back against the wall, intrigued by the boy and nothing else.

"You need to be a kid for crying out loud. Don't worry about acting all proper around me."

"The way I act is the way I am, mister. Someone like you isn't going to change that."

The man looked at the sketches that hung on the wall again, moving close to see the details.

"Well, I'm certain there's a dark side in that innocence you try and project. After looking at this, I'm not buying it, kid."

The pictures were drawn with black, brown, and hunter green crayons. They depicted people in front of a woodsy backdrop with the cabin he was in behind them. These people had deformed faces and looked back at him with a tangible hate.

"What has you so pissed off?" the man said with a nod.

Keir shrugged. "I'm not mad about anything, mister. I just like to draw what I see."

"You see these things?"

"All the time."

The man's facial expression morphed from disgust into a look of curiosity as he inspected what he saw. "Not that I'm complaining, but why is everything so morbid for a boy of the cloth?"

"I told you that you have me confused with someone else, mister."

The man didn't hear Keir's response. In the background of one of the pictures, although difficult to see at first, the likeness of a child was set back in the trees. It looked like he was trying to hide, to use the vegetation as cover. But his youth made him careless and he stood exposed. His eyes were dots of red and were piercing. The man in the suit backed away.

"Don't let them frighten you," Keir said. "That's what yours look like."

He eyed the boy, confused. "My what?"

"That one in the background isn't mature enough to hate you back yet. He's still afraid of you. He sees you as an abuser and that is why I made his eyes red. He cries a lot and knows if you were given enough time, he'd grow into something menacing like the ones in the front."

The man wavered. "I think you've been locked inside this cabin for far too long."

"That might be true, mister, but what you see here—" he pointed at the pictures "—are all yours. You should take them down, sit at the table, and study them and maybe even tell them how sorry you are. It might help you later on."

"Help me with what?"

"What is to come, of course," Keir said and turned with a smile, focusing his attention on the contents of the box again.

"What did they do to you, kid?"

"I think you should be asking yourself what it is you did to them."

"To the things in the picture?" He laughed.

"What's so funny, mister?"

"I'm supposed to make sense of monsters dreamed up from the mind of a child who's been brainwashed by his preacher daddy?"

"Yes, you should believe they are real."

The man laughed again, this time louder, mocking the child.

"Laugh all you want, mister. I'm only trying to help you."

Keir dug through the box in haste. Stuffed animals, Matchbox cars, superheroes, and all types of playthings he scattered about the room without care.

"Finally," he said and took possession of a wrinkled brown paper bag near the bottom of the chest. He held it up as if it were a trophy. "Twyla must have cleaned up my room while I was sleeping." He opened the bag and reached down inside. The paper crunched and the contents jingled. "Now we can play."

"Hey, kid?"

Keir looked at the man, a smile parting his lips. His little teeth were crooked and had wide gaps.

"It's time for you to stop the nonsense. Where am I and how do I get out of here?"

Keir's smile faded and he chuckled. He took his hand out of the bag, folded the ends down and shifted his childlike curiosity towards the man, and settled with a smile. "You're not allowed to leave. That's why I suggested we play a game. It'll help pass the time."

"This isn't a game and I'm not smiling. Now put your stupid bag away and tell me how to get out of here."

Keir's eyes welled with tears. "Is this how you speak to children and show your appreciation to someone who's trying to help you?"

"I've entertained you and your nonsense long enough. I've got to get out of here."

"It's no wonder you're here," Keir said and wiped his eyes. "Nothing I've said to you is nonsense, mister. Not one word of it."

The man ran taut fingers through his hair. "I find myself in the middle of nowhere running for my life with a pack of crazy people chasing me. I get away from them because I happened upon this cabin and now I find myself in a room with a kid who thinks this is a game."

"I don't think this is a game, mister. This—" he rattled the bag "—is a game and we should sit at the table and play."

The man walked to Keir, towering over him. "You're starting to get on my nerves."

"That's too bad because we could have had some fun together."

The man tore a picture off the wall, wiped his shoes with it, and crumpled it up. "Have fun with you? You have these creepy pictures hanging all over your walls. They look like the things outside and I feel like they're staring at me." He tossed it on the floor.

Keir looked at the balled up paper and then back at the man. "You shouldn't disregard them like that."

"I studied it and they're ugly."

"No they're not! You need to apologize!"

"You talk about the things in these pictures as if they're alive!"

"They're not things and they're not going to stand for you doing that to their images. They need to be remembered."

"I'm in a room with a kid as creepy as his drawings," the man said.

"They've suffered for a long time, mister."

"Ah," the man in the suit said and kicked the crumpled paper across the floor. "Maybe you should invite them in and have them pick it up? I'm getting out of here." He went to the door, grabbed the handle, and pulled on it with all his might. But the door didn't budge. "What the hell?" He yanked harder, straining, but to no gain.

"You're not going to be able to open that," Keir said. "As much as we don't like it, you're going to have to stay in here with me. Maybe we should just sit at the table like I suggested." He shook the bag and it rattled. "I have something for us to play together and it's really fun. You might've played it when you were a kid. Maybe we can talk, too, if that'll make you feel better."

The man's shoulders slumped and he rubbed his face. He looked around the room and Keir took the opportunity to sit at the table. He began to trace carvings that were etched into the thick wood tabletop by prior guests. The words *I'm in Hell* were jagged and deep as if each guest had bore their frustration into the wood as they awaited their release from this side of the cabin.

"You better open that door, kid."

"I can't do that," Keir said. "It's impossible."

The man lurched at Keir and the boy flinched. "Yeah, you're not ready for someone like me. Let me out right now before I make you."

"I can't do that, mister," Keir said, cautious. "The door is locked from the other side. The moment I shut that door, I locked us inside without a chance of getting out on our own."

The man turned with a jerk and placed a foot on the wall and pulled on the door handle, using his body weight as leverage. He gave up, exhausted.

"How is that possible?"

"Why won't you listen to me?" Keir said.

"It's just a door."

"Yes, it's just a door and Twyla has to open it."

"I don't understand."

"You should sit down for a while. It'll help you save your energy. In the meantime we can get to know each other, mister."

The man's face turned as red as his suit. "Stop calling me mister! My name is—"

"I know what your name is," Keir said and continued to trace each letter with his finger. "But Twyla and I call you the broken man. The things I know about you are sad and what I see before me is even sadder."

The man clenched his fists. "I'm going to break the damn door down if you don't open it up!"

"Go ahead and try," Keir said. "But you can't get out that way. Many who have come before you have tried, but no one has been able to do it."

The man looked at the door and the seam all around it. He noticed broken fingernails on the floor and claw marks ingrained into the floor and jamb.

"What the hell is this?"

"I tried telling them, too. I told them they couldn't open that door, but they didn't listen."

"I've got to get out of here," the man said and lowered his shoulder and charged the door. Bouncing back and flopping onto the floor, he grabbed his shoulder and writhed.

"Are you OK, mister?"

The man was slow to stand.

"There's no reason for you to do that again. It's pointless and you're going to keep hurting yourself unnecessarily."

Tap. Tap. Tap.

Three faint knocks came from the corner of the room near the toy chest.

"What was that?"

"Nothing," Keir said and stood. He picked at his fingernails, suddenly nervous. "This old cabin makes a lot of noise so don't pay it any attention."

Tap. Tap. Tap.

"Well that didn't sound like nothing to me. It sounds like someone is knocking."

"You need to know that your being here is the most important thing to the man in the other room," Keir said.

"What man?"

Keir stared at the man in the red suit. "He's on the other side of the cabin, talking with Twyla as you're here talking with me. At least that's what you're supposed to be doing instead of arguing with me."

"Why are you telling me about that other man? Who is he?"

Keir opened the bag. "We can talk about that, but what's important is that you two stay separated until the right time." He spilled the contents on the table. Jacks clattered around and a small rubber ball rolled towards the edge. Scooping it up before it fell, he looked at the man with a big smile and showed him the ball. "Did you see how fast I was? I'm like a superhero."

"I'm not here to play with you, kid!"

"What are you going to do, stand there all night and keep prying at a door you can't open?" Keir said, bounced the ball, and snatched a jack off the table.

The man kicked the door repeatedly. "Just open this damn door!"

Keir bounced the ball a second time and swiped two jacks off the table, paying the man no mind.

"Listen, kid," he said and grabbed Keir's shoulder. "I said to open the goddamn door so I can talk to someone about where I am and how I can get the hell out of here."

Keir shrugged off his grip. "Don't ever touch me again, mister. If I told Twyla you just did that, she'd throw you out of the house and let you deal with those things outside all by yourself." He bounced the ball again and grabbed three jacks. "And I don't think you'd like that."

The man swept his hand across the table and scattered the jacks all around the small room. He moved his face close to Keir's. "Go ahead and tell her!"

Keir folded his arms. "You better help me pick up my jacks or I'm not going to play with you."

The man laughed. "There ain't no way in hell I'm helping you pick anything up." He drove a stiff finger into the boy's chest. "Now tell me how to get out of here."

Keir rubbed at the sting the poking finger left behind. "We could have had a lot of fun together while we waited. But you're making this more difficult than it has to be."

"I told you I'm not here to play with you."

Tap. Tap. Tap.

The box jiggled.

"Did you see that?" the man said and hurried to the chest.

"I wouldn't pay any attention to that, mister."

"Well, I'm not you."

He slid the box away from the wall, revealing a trap door.

"Don't open that," Keir said.

The man moved without hesitation. He lifted a small handle on the door and gave it a tug. The hinges whined and a dark hollow wafted stale air that made him cover his nose and mouth with his lapel. Footprints in the dirt below showed him someone had been down there recently.

"It's a passageway," the man said. "I knew there had to be a way out of here."

He took a candle off one of the shelves and eased himself into the cavity.

8

VANITY

The past.

Leo's attention shifted from the sign in the window to his reflection in the glass. In light cast from the overhead streetlamp, he came nose to nose with his ghostly image. Studying the details of his reflection with a focus he hadn't had in a long time, a range of emotions overcame him. Concern came first as a bloody, puffed-up face made him unrecognizable—even to himself—and the severity of his injuries invited a closer look. Anger was quick to come because the idea that someone would do this to him was outrageous. But a sense of guilt and shame dominated because deep inside he knew he deserved it. What he had become and the lengths he went through to conceal it made everyone around him unessential. And from what he could see, that included himself.

"There's nothing good about you," he muttered and raised his good hand to what he saw to wipe the window for a better look.

"Nothing!"

The other half of his face, where he suffered no injury, was white and the veins were dark, making the poison that flowed within easy to see. His expression was pulled down into a scowl and his cheekbones were rosy lumps. Sad eyes that were sunken into a pit of misery cried for help. But the calls went unheard. Confined and forced to endure terrible choices made by whatever it was that controlled them, they blinked hard. Beaten down into something he despised and even wanted to resist, he whimpered. Sick, blackish rings around the eyes were another telltale sign that the sickness within had full control and he could do nothing to escape its oppressive rule.

As he stared, dots of rain speckled the glass, distorting the image, making one half of his face appear as though it was melting and the other half appeared deformed.

Engrossed, he wanted to touch what he saw but when he lifted his other hand he winced and cried out in pain. He stumbled around and tried to aid the bad arm with the good one, but that initial spark of pain ignited everything that was wrong with him and he wished Saint Nick hadn't taken his gun away.

"I'd use it right now," he growled. "End this once and for all."

"Are you all right?" the soft voice of a man behind him said.

Standing upright and pushing back the pain, Leo looked at the man and tried to hide what he was feeling. His arm dangled uselessly at his side and he could feel blood seeping out of the puncture wound on his gut, filling his waistband.

Wearing a full collar shirt and cassock, the man had a gentle face that was outlined by a neatly trimmed white beard. He appeared to be in his fifties and had a gaze that seemed to peer right into Leo's damaged soul.

"Yeah, I'm OK," Leo said, and stricken with pain, he looked at the glass again. The beast was gone and was replaced by the sadness he didn't want to see.

"Your face, child, is cut badly and it's really swollen," the pastor said and removed his outer shirt. "Here, hold this to your face to stop the bleeding."

Leo patted his waist in search of the pack and only found blood. He stiffened. "No, no, no!" he said and pounded the glass, leaving a bloody smear. Pacing with heavy footsteps, he stomped through puddles and stared down the blackened alleyway.

"Are they the ones who did this to you?" the pastor said, moving forward and dabbing Leo's face with his shirt.

"No," he said, trying to figure out how to get the contents of his bag back.

"Your wounds need to be tended to. Whatever is down that alleyway is trouble for you and you should stay away. Don't you think that's a wise suggestion?"

Saint Nick had his waist pack and that meant he had his pipe, too.

"We need to get you some help," the pastor said.

How was he going to use what Saint Nick gave him?

"Are you hearing me, son?"

"I'm not your son and I'm fine," Leo said and pulled away. "I don't have anything for you, Priest." Leo tapped his pocket and felt his tension ease when he touched the rectangle shape of his Zippo lighter. Confident he would be able to find something he could use to get high from something someone had left behind in most any of the stairwells around the neighborhood, he couldn't wait to just get away and forget everything.

"I'm a pastor actually."

"What?" Leo said, annoyed that this guy was distracting him.

"Pastor Stephen Grant," he said with a smile and offered Leo his hand. "I saw you reading the sign I placed in the window. I would like to offer you some food and a place to rest if you don't mind the offer."

Leo ignored the extended hand.

"I don't need your charity, Priest, Pastor or whatever the hell you are."

"It's an act of kindness, not pity. You need a decent meal. You're entitled to take care of yourself, free yourself from your burdens for a little while."

"I think you're on the wrong side of town."

The pastor smiled and bowed. "I go where the Lord guides me."

"I just want to be left alone," Leo said and turned his back to the pastor.

"Perhaps some other time when you feel the need? Even if it is just to talk."

"I doubt that will ever happen."

"That's OK. The offer stands anytime you might have the need. I believe we met for a reason and hope you will remember how much the Lord loves you."

"No one can love what I've become."

"He loves you more now than ever. If you stop and listen, you'll hear Him calling you."

"What I hear is disturbing and I would do almost anything to shut it up."

"Perhaps we should talk then? Would you like to go inside now? I can get you something to eat if you're hungry and get you some dry clothes and clean your wounds."

"I said I wanted to be left alone."

"Perhaps tomorrow then? The Lord is patient and I'm a great listener."

"Talking with you wouldn't fix what's wrong with me."

"Maybe if you tried to understand it, your troubled soul will find a way out of the darkness and into the light."

Leo snickered. "I was fine right where you found me, Pastor."

"A dark alleyway with scheming men is no place to be, young man. Look at what they did to you."

"You should be careful. If they knew you were watching them, they'd kill you. And someone like me would kill you for what you might have in those donation baskets."

"Maybe you would. I'm not worried and I would gladly give you what I had if that's what you needed. That is, as long as it was going to good use and not to those men in the back of the alleyway. All you would need to do is ask."

"Ahh," Leo said, bothered by the old man who stood next to him. The hankering for a hit was growing stronger with each passing moment.

"Either way," the pastor said. "I'm glad we met. I'll be serving breakfast between six and nine a.m. and lunch between noon and two here at the pantry."

"Your sign needs to be updated."

The pastor read the sign. "So it does," he said with a wet smile. He locked the door to the storefront and walked away, saying, "God bless you, son. Jesus loves you and died for your sins. Humble yourself and ask for forgiveness before it is too late."

Leo waited a moment and glanced over his shoulder. His heart burst with the need to confess, to release his culpability. But his desire to stifle the domineering voice inside was stronger. Removing the small plastic baggie from his pocket, he walked in the opposite direction as the pastor, hoping to forget he ever met him.

9

THE TUNNEL

Present day.

"As much as it kills me to do this, I don't think I'll be able to move around in there with this on," the man in the suit said. He took his jacket off.

"You shouldn't be in that hole to begin with, mister."

"Here," the man said and held the jacket up. "Take it and hang it on the back of one of them chairs, would you?"

"You can't be serious about crawling into that hole."

"I'm very serious."

"Don't you think it odd there's a trap door and a hidden passageway underneath my toy box and whatever made that sound is nowhere to be found?"

"I find everything about this place to be odd. Besides, this might be the only way for me to get out of here."

"I told you that you can't leave here, mister."

"No, what you said was that I can't open the door. You didn't say anything about this."

"Well, I am now. Going in there is worse than any bad idea you might have had."

"Maybe you don't mind being stuck inside this room, but I do. I have people I need to see."

"That's your problem right there, mister. You don't listen. You think I'm some dumb kid cooped up in a cabin in the middle of nowhere and that I don't know any better. But I do."

"I heard everything you had to say. But I'm not about to sit around and wait for whatever is waiting for me outside. Maybe you should come with me—it might be your only chance to get away from that daddy of yours."

Keir sighed. "I don't want to get away, mister. What I have here is way better than whatever is down there. If you go crawling into that hole, then you're going to do it alone."

"No skin off of my back," the man said with a shrug. "I don't mind getting dirty when I have to. Now, take this, would you?" He shook the coat.

Keir took it and the man picked up the candle he'd set down, lifted his pants at the thighs, and squatted. He looked into the rounded tunnel carved deep into the earth, pitching downwards at a slight angle; it faded into a pitch black dot. "Wherever this goes, it has to be better than being stuck in this room."

"You don't know that," Keir said, standing over the hole, peering down with worry. "At least being inside here gives you protection from what you know is outside."

The man looked at Keir. "That's where I've got the conflict. I'm worried about what's inside the cabin more than what might be down here in this hole."

Keir turned away with a sigh and hung the coat on the back of a chair. "I don't suppose I can change your mind then?"

The man studied the hole. Shoe impressions in the soil faded into the black and the ground was dry and packed tight. People had traveled this tunnel many times before and some of the tracks looked fresh. He raised the candle to try and spread the light, but the narrow passageway swallowed the glow, revealing ten, maybe fifteen feet tops before it faded into nothingness.

"I'm going, kid," the man said and crawled into the tunnel. As he looked ahead, protecting the flame, the burrow seemed to stretch on forever. Onward he moved, brushing away the dirt that stuck to his hands and pausing long enough to raise the candle to see what he could find. The vanishing point always looked the same: an uninviting black dot that insisted he keep moving forward.

"You're going to make me work for whatever it is you have to give me," he said and crawled. "I can respect that." One hand moved ahead, one hand held the candle, and his knees dug into small rocks. "I just want you to know that I don't quit easily."

Onwards he went, ever mindful of his precious candlelight, hoping to find a way out of this tunnel. The musty smell of the soil had become strong, but the air remained still, flattening his hope that there was a way out. He knew if there was no air movement, then that meant there was no clear exit.

"I make it through that dreaded forest without a blemish to my wardrobe only to find myself here, on my hands and knees, crawling through the dirt, ruining my favorite suit!"

"Please, come back, mister!"

Keir's voice was far off but the desperation in his tone was easy to hear. Having no time to acknowledge it, the fast approach of a howling wind rushed past the man, blowing dirt into his face and snuffing his candle. Encased in a terrifying ebon embrace, his eyes stung and he could feel the darkness come alive . . . "It's going to drag me away! Help me!" he shouted and hoped the boy could hear him and would come to offer his help. He looked back, searching for his point of entry into the tunnel. In the far distance he could see a dim blush of light he wasn't even sure was really there. The darkness was a bitter black and completely silent and had a terror about it that was indescribable.

"Keep that door open," the man shouted and tried to turn around, but the channel had become too narrow.

"No," he grunted and thrashed as the walls around him started to crumble. Just then a sound made him look forward. A bright spark of light turned his need to escape into curiosity. He watched the glow and was amazed. Encouraged to move farther into the earth, he scurried along on his hands and knees, sinking into the loosening soil as he progressed, his focus firmly on the light ahead. Strangely, the flame danced high in the air.

As he neared, he noticed that a long root poking through the dirt ceiling was on fire. Beyond the flame and up high, something small and fast scurried along the dangling root system. Using tiny hands and pincer type feet, a small creature dropped from the ceiling and glided to the ground with open, arching wings that flapped gently. The being stood hunched with its head below its shoulder line. It came forward with quick, silent steps, cautious in every way.

"What the hell?" the man said and flicked dirt at it and backed away.

"Shh," the thing said and held a finger against its lipless mouth. It had an eerie voice and moved sporadically, jerking and then stopping and then moving again.

The man paused and looked at the thin tiny, goblin-like creature. It had a bone-like mask for a face and devilish red eyes. Giving pause beneath the burning root, it skillfully danced and posed with open arms when it finished.

The man laughed and the imp bowed. The scales on the skin reminded the man of a reptile and he stared, expecting a flicking black tongue. Instead, the imp stomped a foot and carved an X into the dirt with its heel.

"What's that?" the man said and was drawn forward. He looked at the mark and, not understanding its meaning, he returned his gaze back at the imp.

It pointed at the X and pretended to dig. The flame overhead dimmed and the imp tapped his wrist impatiently.

"The light?" the man said. "I'm running out of time?"

The imp nodded and the man hurried forward and clawed at the cold moist ground with haste. Buried less than a foot below the surface was a metal box. Removing it from the hole, he brushed away the dirt and saw an engraving of an imp on top of the box. Upon opening the hinged lid he discovered a rectangular metal object. He examined it, picked it up and found that, like the box, it was icy cold. Opening the flip top lid, he identified it as a Zippo lighter.

Turning the flint wheel with his thumb and creating a spark that produced a flame, he lit a root on fire only moments before the original flame died. The imp applauded, turned away, and retreated farther into the tunnel, waving the man on.

"Wait, who are you?" the man said and followed the imp. Pausing to light every root that poked through the dirt ceiling about every twenty feet or so, the imp watched and waited and then led him farther into the tunnel.

The passageway curved left and right and the soil got softer, held a seeping cold, and became more difficult to traverse. And it seemed the farther they traveled, the sparser the roots became and the more difficult they were to light on fire.

"Wait a minute. Hold on," the man said, giving in to the cold that numbed him down to the bone. He felt as though he'd been crawling for an hour, maybe more, and he needed rest.

But the imp kept going.

"Are you leading me to the exit?" the man said, and his triceps shook with fatigue. His palms and knees were bruised, aching under the weight of his body. "I can't," he said and rested on his backside. His neck bent awkwardly, the tunnel noticeably much smaller now.

The imp returned to the man and crouched. It looked into the black distance and pointed, firm in the message it was trying to send.

"It's that way, is that what you're trying to tell me?" the man said.

The imp nodded and hurried along.

"Are we close?" the man said and got on all fours. He tried to keep pace with the small creature but his rest made him realize how tired his muscles were. Pausing, he searched for another root to light.

"Wait!" the man shouted, straining his voice. "Something ain't right. Everything is soaking wet and I'm getting confused. I just need to rest a minute to figure this out."

Trembling uncontrollably, one after the other, the roots behind him dimmed and slowly died, giving the darkness back its cave.

"No, no, no!" the man said, and he tried to turn the wheel on the lighter but was unable to feel his fingers. Dropping the lighter, he saw the blackness take over again, and it was wicked. Panic made him forget his pain and he started to hyperventilate. He raked his fingers through the muck, frantic to find the lighter; he knew that small flame could be the difference between life and death.

Skritch.

The flame came to life and the imp held the lighter out. It hovered in the center of the tunnel and gracefully flapped its wings just a few feet away from the man.

"Oh, thank you," the man said. The tiny source of light filled him with hope. He shivered and reached out to take the lighter, his bottom jaw banging into the top, making his teeth click. The imp backed away and flipped the lid closed.

"Don't do that!"

Skritch.

The flame came to life again and the imp had moved deeper into the tunnel.

"Please," the man whimpered. "Come back. I can't go any farther."

The imp held the lighter out, beckoning him forward with his other hand.

The tremble within the man had become so bad he could hardly get his body to move. But with one last push and great resolve, he crawled with his focus firmly on the flame, believing that if he were to reach the lighter, the imp would give it to him and he would be able to return to Keir and his room.

But the tunnel pitched down and it was steep. Straining his tired muscles beyond their ability, he fell forward, collapsing face first into the mud. He slid down the embankment and came to an abrupt stop, settling a mere two feet away from the lighter. Extending his arms and sinking his fingers into the mud, he pulled himself forward a few more inches. As he got close enough to reach the lighter, the walls crumbled on top of him, pinning him down.

The imp approached and watched him with an unnerving curiosity. It poked at him before it took two steps past the man's reach and planted the lighter in the dirt. The flame burned with an abating orange and blue glow. The imp danced again, bowed, and without a sound, it departed.

"Get back here!" the man attempted to shout but could only manage a dry wheeze. Trapped with no way out, he wriggled in a last ditch effort to loosen the grip of the muddy hand that held him. But the walls and ceiling caved and squeezed the breath from his lungs. And strangely, the only thing that came to mind was how he had been warned by the boy not to come down here. But he hadn't listened because he thought he was just a stupid kid, raised in some backwards cabin deep in the woods, lonely and desperate for companionship. How the man wished he had him around right now.

More of the tunnel collapsed, burying his head with moist earth and pressing him down with a weight that would slowly smother him to death.

10

TOUGH LOVE

The past.

Leo hurried up three steps and lost his footing. Falling into a closed door with a clumsy bang, he bounced off and flopped to the floor. He had the need to rub something that hurt but couldn't identify what; he laughed and managed to get himself into a sitting position. The dizzy world came back into focus and he searched for whatever it was he had tripped on. A welcome mat on the ground in front of him held his attention.

Coconut fibers with bold black letters written cursively were intended to make visitors believe the declaration was true.

"Yeah, that's funny," he said and tossed the mat into the bushes. What that mat said was a lie. He was anything but welcome and was about to prove that.

Using the door jamb and wall to help him stand, he steadied himself. The porch light flicked on and he squinted at the sudden blink of bright light.

Pulling on his hood, he retreated into the darkness and watched the door. There was a certain pleasure in this moment. He anticipated how good he was going to feel when he saw the look of surprise on his father's face and his inability to form a word. To witness that struggle would be monumental. It would show the chink in his father's armor and would expose the weakness he didn't show anyone. Always being in control was something his father worked very hard at, and he was good at it, too.

"Leo?" his father said, the surprise not there. Stiff with disappointment—that was the last thing Leo wanted to hear.

"Hello, Father," Leo said and tried to hide his own displeasure. He needed to find another way through the thick, tall barriers his father had erected and managed to keep up for so long. Maybe if he could see his father's facial expression and how it contradicted his tone of voice, but the obscurity of the unlit interior of the house behind him concealed him.

"What are you doing here, Leo?"

The words were firm and infuriating, but Leo had a final play to make. Pulling off his hood and stepping forward, he lifted his chin to the light and he heard his father gasp. The lumps and gashes on his face from the beating Saint Nick and his henchmen left behind were almost worth hearing that. But his father said nothing.

"I'm in need of a favor from you, Dad."

His father didn't reply, and for Leo, the silence that had inserted itself was far worse than being scolded for showing up uninvited or even being questioned about what had happened to him. Inexplicable rage, much like the kind he carried around inside, would have been easier to combat than this. Instead, his father was disappointed in him the same way Leo was in himself and that was one of the things he had tried so hard to hide from.

"Do you have any idea what time it is?" his father asked.

"No," Leo said and looked over his shoulder. Night hugged the neighborhood and everything was still. The rain had stopped, and although his clothing was still wet, it appeared as though things had begun to dry. At least that was what the ground around his feet made him believe. His gaze shifted and he wondered if the overhang he stood underneath had protected the area from the storm. He looked at his father. "What time is it?"

"Are you high again, Leo?"

"What does it matter? I didn't come here to hear your shit, Dad!"

"And I didn't expect my son to become a junkie and someone's punching bag. I don't know who you are anymore and haven't for a long time. Why don't you take your problems and go?"

"I'm not leaving. I have nowhere else to go."

"I'm going to call the police."

"Do you always have to be such an asshole?"

"Watch your mouth," his father said and stepped outside. His eyes were wide and red, puffy from sleep. "It's three o'clock in the morning, Leo. The neighbors are sleeping and I don't need you causing a scene and waking them. You've already caused enough problems around here."

"Why do you think I give a damn about the neighbors and what they think?"

"I know you don't."

"You're damn right I don't."

"That's because you only care about yourself and that attitude is what helped turn you into this." He took his glasses out of a pocket of the thick robe he was wrapped in and put them on. He looked at his son through thick lenses, his reddened eyes unblinking.

"What are you looking at? You turned me into this. Can you see that through your glasses?"

"I had nothing to do with this."

Leo laughed. "Yeah, sure, you can keep telling yourself that."

"What happened to your face, Leo?"

He shrugged. "What, all of a sudden you care? Besides, what does it matter?"

Leo pulled his hood up. It was much better there and it was easier to dodge the questions he didn't like.

"Can you even feel that?" his father asked. "Your face is a mess."

Leo looked at his feet and the ground undulated and he staggered.

"You're high right now, Leo. Your thoughts are all over the place and you can barely stand."

Leo clenched his fists and fixed his father with a bitter glance. "What I am is freezing cold because my clothes are wet. I've been out in the rain for days and have barely eaten. Do you care about that?"

His father looked at him, unwilling or unable to answer. But Leo would force the answer out of him.

"Maybe I can come inside and dry off for a little while? Do you have anything for me to eat?"

"No," his father said and kept looking at him. It was if his eyes were trying to pry into the shadow of Leo's hood and pull out a truth about his son that he was never going to get.

Leo turned away. "I don't like it when you look at me like that."

"How am I supposed to look at you, Leo? Am I supposed to be proud of what I see?"

Now it was Leo's turn to stand in silence.

"If you can only see how much you've changed since the last time I saw you."

"I'm surviving, aren't I?"

"You're barely existing, Leo."

"Well, you're the one who told me to stay away."

"You're here now, so you didn't. Why did you come back?"

"Because I need your help."

"No, Leo," he said and shifted. "I've done all I can for you. You need to leave and never come back."

Beyond the door, concealed by the shadows of the darkened house, Leo saw the frail image of his mother. She was shaking and crying and it broke his heart.

"Mother?" Leo said and went to step past his father.

His father placed a hand on Leo's chest. "What do you think you're doing?"

"Mom's in there and she's crying! I want to make sure she's all right."

His father looked over his shoulder and back at Leo. "Get out of here. I'll give you a few minutes' head start before the police come and look for you. They've been looking for you for weeks and want to ask you some questions. I hope they put you away for a long time. Maybe you can get some help."

"I don't care about the police and their questions. I just want to get inside so I can check on Mom. If you let me do that, I'll leave!"

Leo went to step past his father again but his father refused to move. He snapped his fingers. "I don't know if this is some sick game you're playing, but I don't like it." His expression maddened and he pointed at Leo, his finger close to his face. "You are never allowed to step foot in this house again. You're sick and destructive to everyone and everything around you. I don't want you around me. You remind me of what happened and I can't bear to look at you. Do you get that?"

The thought of shoving his father aside was interrupted by a whimper that came from inside the house.

"Mom?"

Everything went quiet.

"What is wrong with her?" Leo said, and although the darkness concealed the details, he could see she was shaking. "We need to help her!"

"What is wrong with you, Leo?"

He looked at his father and back at his mother. She continued to shake and the sound of her sobbing was disturbing and he needed to help her.

"Look at me, Leo!" his father said.

Leo looked at his father and he thought if madness had a face, he was looking at it. "What is wrong with Mom and why won't you let me help her?"

"Because you can't help her, Leo. You yourself are helpless and cannot hope to offer anyone help. Don't you get that?"

"You've always been unreasonable, but this! You think you can keep me from seeing my own mother!"

His father grabbed for him but couldn't get a hold of the wet clothes.

"Mom?" Leo shouted and shoved his father aside. He saw a glimpse of his mother's flowing nightgown as she hurried into another room.

"Don't you dare put your hands on me!" his father said and managed to back Leo away from the door.

"I didn't mean to. Mom, she's—"

Breathing heavily, his father fixed his glasses and robe and gave into a sob.

Leo smiled.

"You are so lost, Leo. I want you out of here. Do as I ask and never come back. As far as I'm concerned, you're dead to me."

"But I need your help. I need Mom's help and she needs me. I would like dry clothes to put on and to have something to eat."

His father shook his head, his eyes pinpoints of judgment, his lips stretched into a saddened slit. "You get nothing from me, Leo, and you'll certainly get nothing from your mother."

Leo ran taut fingers through his hair and spun as he tried to think.

"I'm not asking you, I'm telling you to get out of here."

The tone was harsh and deeply unsettling.

"How could you be so mean? I'm your son."

"No, not anymore. You changed that a half a year ago."

"You saying that doesn't make it so. I am your flesh and blood."

"That might be," his father said and touched his chest over his heart. "But what you've done to this says something else entirely. And it wants you to go in the worst way."

You need money. Get it in promise of going.

"Fine, I'll leave," Leo said. "I just need you to give me some money to help me get through the next few days and you'll never see me again."

"I don't have anything for you."

"I can't go back out there. I owe someone money and if I don't pay, they're going to do something far worse to me than a beating."

"I don't know what to say other than I don't have a single cent to pay for what you do. You've managed to figure out how to get high this long, I'm sure you can figure out how to get yourself past this."

"No," Leo said and shook his head. It made him dizzy. "This is different. This is bigger than getting past the moment."

"How much do you owe?"

"Four thousand."

His father raised a brow. "That's a lot of money, Leo. How did you manage to create such a debt?"

"They're holding me responsible for everything that was taken."

"What do you remember about that night?"

He whimpered. "I try not to think about it."

"Maybe that's part of your problem and you should think about it. It might help you come to terms with what happened and not chase every shadow you see moving."

He shook his head. "I don't want to. It's too painful and I've been working too hard to forget."

"I can see that, Leo. Every moment of it."

"You say that like I'm the only one to blame."

His father licked his lips. "I wrestle with my own demons, too, and often wonder if I'd done things differently how it would have changed the outcome. I allowed you to stay around us when I knew you were up to no good. I ignored what I saw and hoped if I treated you with kindness and love you wouldn't be so defiant and you'd listen to your mom and me."

"I couldn't because you brought home a disease and gave it to me. I never told you that, but it's true."

"What are you talking about, Leo?"

"Who was that man you and that doctor were so obsessed with?"

"Who?"

"The one with the curse?"

"Alister?"

He nodded. "Yes, him. You brought home whatever he had and it attached itself to me."

His father heaved a sigh. "Oh, Leo."

"I would hear its voice and it would frighten me. Drugs were the only things that would keep it quiet."

"Your drug use has made you paranoid and desperate. Fantasy and reality have been blurred to you and if you don't stop using it, it is going to kill you."

"I'm not one of your patients!"

"No, you're not," his father said and turned away. "You're something far more complicated."

Leo looked at him wordlessly.

"Have you thought about that phone call you got that day? I'm talking about the one that got you out of the house and left your mother alone?"

"I said I try my hardest not to think about that."

"It's like I said. You should think about it because something about that day doesn't sit right with me," his father said, turned away, and walked toward the open door. He stepped inside the house. "Maybe you should think about that when you sober up some." He started to close the door.

This is your last chance! Get some money.

Leo stuck his foot inside and stopped the door from closing. He rammed his shoulder into the door with all of his might and his father fell to the floor, hard. Leo kicked him several times and his father shouted out in pain.

"Stay down," Leo said.

Leo went to the cherry wood foyer table and pulled the drawer open. He spotted his father's billfold, took it, and ran out of the house. Stuffing it into his pants pocket, he continued to run until he couldn't run anymore. And soon, he forgot the reason why he started running in the first place.

11

THE BOOK

Present day.

Twyla held Hamartia's hand and walked her towards the door. The beast growled at Leo, showing her fangs as she passed him, backing him away. He bumped into the table and turned to catch whatever was falling. But everything was in its place. The thick book Twyla had been so protective of was left on her chair, placed down and presumably forgotten about while she escorted the monster outside. A silk bookmark hung out of the charred pages and dangled, swaying gently and inviting him over, beckoning him like a wiggling finger.

Leo looked over his shoulder and saw Twyla and Hamartia. They still held onto each other as they neared the door, no longer paying attention to him. He carefully moved the book to the tabletop and set it down, careful not to make a sound.

"Don't mind him, dear," Twyla said to the beast. "His time is almost done here and that means your wait is almost over. You're next."

The thing whimpered.

"I'm sorry, I know it seems like a long time to go, but it's not," Twyla said and touched Hamartia gently. "He only has two logs left now. Like the others, they'll burn away and he'll be gone before you know it."

Leo looked at the stack to verify the claim. There were only two logs left and the fire burned big, consuming the wood inside quickly.

"It's time for you to go," Twyla said.

The conversation between Twyla and the beast continued to distract Leo. He watched them and reeled as Twyla's old wrinkled hand lovingly caressed the side of the monster's malformed face. Her gnarled fingers swept over blemished skin and wiped away tears.

"Don't cry, sweetheart," Twyla said. "I know you've been through a lot and I wish there was something I could do to make you feel better, but I can't." She giggled. "But maybe you'd like to say goodbye to Leo?"

Hamartia turned fast and growled at Leo, backing him up. He bumped into Twyla's stool and fell into the seat. The beast grabbed the remaining two logs and tossed them into the fire. She returned to Twyla.

"There now, I hope that helped you feel better," Twyla said and took the beast by the arm.

Leo fingered the book, stroking the bookmark and watching the women interact. He didn't trust that thing Twyla was with and hated the way she taunted him. She fed the fire all of his logs, shortening his time.

"Go ahead, go find your group and stay with them," Twyla said and continued to pet Hamartia. "Your time for the hunt is near."

Hamartia leaned into the touch, basking in it for a moment before turning away and stepping out the door without further protest. Leo watched her push her way through the misshapen crowd gathered outside, waiting for him like a lynch mob.

Leo moved fast, flipping the book open to the marked page and a picture of a gazelle running from a lion inside a dense forest had been created with a careful hand and sharp, precise lines. Delicately woven into the pattern of trees on the top of the page, and although difficult to make out, he managed to decipher letters that were hidden.

Leopold Conroy

He looked at Twyla and her attention remained on the crowd outside the door. He turned the stiff page and the edges crumbled. Pictured on the next page was the gazelle downed in a clearing with the lion hovering around it, ready to eat.

"One, two, three," Twyla said and stood on her toes, distracting Leo again. He watched her shift and point as she counted how many creatures she could see. "Four, five, six, seven, eight, nine . . . my," she said. "There are far too many of you out here to count, waiting for Leo. Be patient. You'll all be reunited soon."

Leo motioned to close the book, but the fancy dips and curves of the drawing demanded further study. Maybe they held a clue as to why he was there, who exactly the beasts outside were, and ultimately how he could escape them.

"Go on now, all of you, go and get some rest. It won't be long now," Twyla said, and she shut the door and engaged the locks.

There, at the bottom of the page, hidden in the tall grass were the words: *Leo's cause of—*

"What are you doing?" Twyla said and closed the heavy cover. Leo gasped and withdrew his hand, the pages slapping shut with a thump.

"You scared me."

"You shouldn't be looking in there."

"Why is that?"

"Because it doesn't belong to you."

"Why is my name in there?"

"Because it is."

Leo huffed. "Why?"

"Why?" Twyla said and scoffed. "Is that all you know how to say?"

"My name was in those pictures. Who drew them?"

"Ah," Twyla said and paused. She groaned deep in her throat.

"What is it?"

She shook her head. "It's nothing."

"You're not being truthful. What is it?"

Her eyes looked glossy in the firelight.

"It's about whoever drew those pictures in that book, isn't it? You know them?"

She wiped her eyes. "It's a him, and I haven't thought about him in a long time."

"Tell me about him."

"Your fire is raging, you've run out of logs, and your time is running out. Your concern should be on yourself, not on me, and certainly not on whoever wrote that book."

"There's significance to it. Your reaction . . . who wrote it?"

Shaking her head and busying herself by tending to the fire, she shifted the logs around with the poker, positioning them in such a way that it seemed to slow the burn. "You should be doing things like this, not me. My body has been ravaged by time and sometimes the simplest task is a strenuous chore. You just sit there like it's OK to watch an old woman struggle when you can lend a hand. And what do I care about preserving your time here? You've been nothing but trouble."

"I know you try and change the subject to keep from answering questions you might not like. Not this time. I want you to tell me who made that book and why."

She went to speak, but her mouth just hung open as if the words were stuck inside.

"Was it the boy?" Leo said. "Did he do this?"

She shook her head.

"Who then?"

"Someone complicated and special. He's someone who often struggles with his own purpose but has served the greater good." She hobbled over to the book, caressed the cover, and lingered in a conflicted moment of silence.

"I need to know more than that. Who wrote it, Twyla?"

"Someone good enough for me to follow into a godforsaken place like this." She opened the cover of the book and trolled through the pages. "This man volunteered to serve Man and our love bound us, bringing me here with him."

"Bound you how?"

"We had no idea that it would be this consuming and that it would keep us apart for so long."

"Walk out that door and go find him then, I don't care!" Leo shouted, pounding his fist on the book.

"I can't."

"Why the hell did he write that book?"

"He wrote it for me," she said, and a tear fell on a page, smearing the ink, putting a blemish on the perfect drawing.

"Why would my name be in an old book that was authored for you by someone you haven't seen in a long time? How could he possibly know I was going to come here?"

"So I could study it. Get to know the people in there before they arrived."

Leo stood up straight, his mind consumed with the possibilities.

"I've done this for a hundred million lives, maybe more," Twyla said. "The world has become so chaotic and godless that I've lost count and have become stranded here." She closed the book.

"Why did you need to know me?"

"Because it is my job to do so."

He grabbed his chin, wrestling with what he knew and trying to understand what he didn't. "Your purpose here is to study drawings and find hidden messages?"

"The messages aren't hidden to a clear mind, Leo. They're there, in plain sight, intertwined with the story of your life told through pictures."

A lion and a gazelle told the story of his life? It was a ridiculous claim.

"When will this man be returning?"

"I don't know," she said, her sadness palpable. "It has been many years since I saw him. Last time he was here, I remember him telling me how tired he was and how he wished he could find a way to break the bonds that keep us in service of the people. I haven't heard from him since. I'm beginning to worry he might have done something foolish."

"What are you worried he might have done, Twyla?"

"I don't know."

"Is that why I'm here?"

"I don't know how to answer these questions."

"In truth," he said, and pressed his hands on the tabletop. "Now who is he?"

"Even if I were to speak his name you wouldn't know who he was."

"Tell me, dammit!"

"Sariel," she said and held his gaze. "His name is Sariel. Does that name mean anything to you?"

Leo shook his head.

"Of course not," she said and looked away. "He is a tall, handsome man who walks an endless road, performing a thankless task. The last time I saw him we were sorting through his newest compilation. And after he handed me this book he said he had to go, that he had a lot of work to do."

"Tell me, Twyla, why would this Sariel draw those pictures and hide may name in them?"

"To enlighten me so that I might help prepare you. Can't you see your questions have us going in circles?"

Indeed they were. Perhaps a compliment?

"Something about those drawings is exquisite yet unsettling," he said, and pointed at the door. "It has something to do with me and them, doesn't it?"

She nodded. "Yes. It has everything to do with you, the things outside, and the man in the other room."

Leo looked at the fire ravaging the logs like the lion had done to the gazelle. The lion may very well be a representation of the things outside. If that were the case, then he knew his fate. The images he saw disturbed him and he wished he'd never seen them.

"Sariel just sees what is," Twyla said. "That's why he authored that and placed you inside the forest."

Leo whispered Twyla's words back to her, trying to comprehend.

"He needs to keep his focus on those who are worthy of his attention and guides those who are not to me," she said. "I get the damned."

The heat of the flames no longer felt welcoming. They were searing and dangerous. Maybe he could use them to keep the things at bay if he needed to make a run for it . . .

"Am I the gazelle?"

She nodded and the thought he might have it all wrong inspired his next question.

"And the man in there—" he pointed at Keir's room—"is he the lion?"

She nodded again.

"Then who are they?" Leo said, pointing at the door.

Twyla opened the book to the page after the one with the lion hovering over the gazelle. Drawn spectacularly, the lion still hovered over its kill in the clearing, and all around it, hyenas crowded in. They packed in a tight circle in such numbers that the lion appeared as though it had no chance of keeping its kill. Despite its great strength and massive size, it was in danger of being overwhelmed by sheer numbers.

"It seems this night has been difficult for the both of us," she said.

He looked at the picture and searched for the hidden words but it was too complex. "What does it mean?"

"Yes, Leo, what does it mean?" Twyla said. She closed the book and picked it up. "What does any of this mean to a man lost in a forest and happened upon a cabin in this valley?"

She held the book tight against her chest and Leo watched her waddle into the darkened room, her clicking toenails like a tick to the final countdown. She was swallowed by the black veil and he approached the room with caution, careful not to touch the darkness. His desire to stay away from it was as strong as his need to avoid the things that were outside.

"If you truly want answers, then come inside this room with me. The time has come for you to know."

He hesitated, the black barrier like a lid capping secrets he wasn't sure he was ready to face.

12

THE BODY

The past.

You've got to get up.

Leo was kneeling on the floor, staring down at the body he had etched into the cement floor inside his apartment. The voice that commanded him was stuffed somewhere in the back of his head. He reached a shaky hand out and ran his fingers over the jagged scratches.

"Who are you?" he said to the engraving, noticing the tremble had gone through his entire body. He tried to remember when he had made the impression into the floor and why. But there was a gap of time he couldn't remember.

We've worked hard at that.

"I couldn't face it," he said but didn't know why.

So I helped you forget.

Around the top of the head and toward the face, his fingers sank further into the splits and the cement tore at his burnt fingertips. Ignoring the pain, he continued to trace the face and allow his fingers to find what would be the hands, clasped in what he envisioned to be a moment of pleading and prayer. The body was curled in the fetal position and the deep-toothed lines etched into the cement told him it was a moment of great pain and anger.

Get up.

The image of a room that was blistered in carmine red flashed through his mind and he slapped the ground in protest. The need to sit with his creation, to not leave it in a time of need, was strong—so strong that he moved against the commands of the voice within, not fearing its wrath. He needed to understand this.

He settled into a sitting position next to the image of the body. The wet clothes he wore wrapped him in a blanket of cold that he could barely feel; maybe that was how cold his heart had become.

Something hard in his back pocket compelled him to reach for it. He withdrew a wallet and, fascinated, he opened it and stared dumbfounded at his father's driver's license.

See how much money is inside.

Shocked by his discovery, he dropped the wallet. A vague memory of having seen his father recently touched his senses and he chased it.

"You're not welcome here anymore," he could hear his father say. His tone was harsh and judgmental and Leo struggled to understand why.

Because he's a bastard.

Maybe he was. He seemed to care for his work so much more than his own son. He willingly surrounded himself with people who were mentally disturbed and barely paid anyone normal any attention. How could he think he could nurture a child into the world without passing onto his offspring some of the burdens of the people he struggled to care for?

Because he's a damn fool.

He must be because he had become obsessed with a patient cursed with death and he ended up bringing it home and giving it to his son. And when he was told about it, all he could do was deny it. But Leo felt its presence and began having bad dreams that were becoming increasingly strange, making it harder to discern between reality and fantasy. He became desperate to escape them. And that is when he met Saint Nick.

"Maybe this is me," he said with a heavy heart and stared at the image he had scribed into the cement. "Or the part of me that was once good." Having been deprived of love for so long, it lay there on the floor and the only way he could preserve it was to capture it in this illustration.

The wallet.

Leo took the wallet and dug out three one-hundred dollar bills and four twenty dollar bills that were folded on top of some tens and singles. Tossing the wallet aside, he added up how much he had and felt distressed.

"Four hundred twenty-three dollars," he said with a sigh, knowing that wasn't nearly enough to cover what he owed and promised Saint Nick. But it was more than enough to get him his next few highs. "He won't give me any more until I pay that debt."

You're just going to have to face him and convince him otherwise.

Every inch of Leo's body hurt and the idea of having to endure another beating made him whimper. "I can't."

Oh, you will.

"That would be suicide. I don't have enough money."

Catching a shadow out of the corner of his eye, Leo turned fast to see what it was. Nothing was there, but he remembered how his mother had lurked in the shadows as if she were afraid to face him. Maybe she'd followed him home to watch him.

"Why have you forsaken me, Mother?" Leo said, and when the quiet remained, tears streamed down his face. "Is it because of what I've become?"

What does she matter?

"I thought a parent is supposed to love their child no matter what?"

She's no better than him.

"Shh," he said and pressed his hands against his ears. "I don't want to hear you right now. I just need a moment to think."

He rocked back and forth, trying to understand why he was sitting on the floor, suddenly attracted and seemingly attached to his drawing, remembering fragments of a past he tried so hard to forget.

In a snapshot of clarity, he sat up straight as he remembered his father saying, "I want you to think about that phone call you got that day." The words were clear enough as if he were in the room speaking to Leo right now. "I'm talking about the one that got you out of the house to make that drug deal."

There was something behind those words, but whatever the meaning was continued to elude him. The answer was there, somewhere, buried in months of drug abuse and malnutrition. These were all efforts to try and erase the wrongdoings of his past.

I said to get up!

A firm slash of pain deep within his core made him fall over and gag violently. It came again and again making him gasp as he tried to steady himself against the onslaught of sheer agony burning in his stomach. Never in his life had he felt pain so raw and profound. It created sparks of regret and he wanted to beg for mercy but couldn't catch his breath.

To your feet!

Like the flick of a switch, the pain receded and gave him a chance to act in response. Lying on his back, he sucked in air and coughed, deep and whooping. After several moments, he was encased in a silence so perfect it demanded he speak.

"My father was trying to say something to me."

And he is a fool. Forget him.

"But I need to know what it meant," he said.

His gut twisted as if something were inside, moving around with a sharp instrument. He gurgled and a forming pressure behind his eyes made the room blurry. He reached for the hand engraved into the floor, looking for comfort. But the pain intensified and curled his body into the fetal position, mimicking the markings he'd made almost perfectly. And then a massive wave of blackness swept over him and took him away.

* * *

Leo watched his mother maneuver around the kitchen, setting the table for dinner. Her black hair was spiked with gray and lines that surrounded her eyes accented the sadness he hadn't noticed until now.

He saw himself walk into the room and pull open the refrigerator. It seemed odd he would be wearing a hoodie with the hood up inside the house. He looked around inside the refrigerator and began to shove things around on the top shelf.

"Get out of the fridge," his mother said. "We're going to be eating dinner in a little while."

"What are we having?"

"Steak and potatoes."

"That sounds good," he said and continued to rummage around.

"Leo?"

He looked over his shoulder. "Yeah?"

"Take that hood off of your head while you're inside this house. It doesn't need to be on."

He turned his attention back to the contents of the fridge. "I don't want to take it off. I like it."

"Well, I don't and you're in my house. I don't know why you're up all night and sleeping all day long." She placed a fork and steak knife on either side of each of the three plates. "Your father and I have been talking about this and we're concerned. We both agree that you need to get a job."

"I have a job."

"What is it you do?"

"I work."

"Where?"

He shrugged.

"Your father wants to talk to you about your behavior."

Leo pulled up his sagging jeans with a sigh.

"And? It's not like he's ever home to talk to me about anything anyways."

"Hey," she said and pointed at him with a fork. "That's not fair. He works hard to provide for us."

"Yeah, sure," Leo said. "And he talks a lot about that doctor lady."

"Doctor Lee is a coworker of your father's, nothing more."

"If you say so. It doesn't mean I have to like her."

"No, you don't. But you still need to be respectful."

"Whatever, Mom."

"Don't whatever me," she said and leaned against the table. "She only talked to you because your father and I asked her to."

"Why?"

"Because of your behavior. We're concerned about you."

"Why? Because I don't want to be his prodigy in that stupid hospital?"

"No," she said and busied herself by folding napkins. "We're concerned about you because you said you were having bad dreams and you've been acting weird."

"I told you, it felt like Dad brought home that guy's sickness and it . . . attached itself to me."

"That's why we wanted you to talk to Doctor Lee."

"What did she say?"

"That she shares the same concerns as us. Why wouldn't you talk to her?"

"Because I have nothing to say to her."

"She's a doctor, Leo."

"Yeah, for crazy people."

"No one thinks you're crazy. She's a friend of the family and has your best interest in mind."

"Sure, whatever."

"Your father and I have been talking about getting you treatment."

"I just want to be left alone."

"We're not going to leave you alone, Leo."

"Fine. You want to know? That doctor talked to me like I was a patient inside that asylum. It really pissed me off and I feel like you guys are pushing me away."

"We're not meaning to do that."

"Well you are!"

His mother folded her arms across her chest. "I want to ask you something, but I don't want you to get mad. You're up all night and sleep all day. Is there something about the darkness you don't like?"

"I love the darkness, that's what you're not getting," Leo said and slammed the refrigerator door closed.

"I know the doctor put you up to that stupid question because she already asked me that."

"Did she now?"

"Give it a rest, would you, Mom?"

"I don't like it when you speak to me like that, Leo. I'm your mother and it's disrespectful."

"Why are you setting a plate for Dad? You know he's not going to be home in time to join us for dinner and have this big talk. We've already tried this and it didn't work. He has other things to do that are way more important."

"What are you so angry about, Leo?" She moved close to him and reached for his head. "Take that hood off. I haven't seen your face in weeks."

"Don't touch me," he said and pulled on the rim of his hood. It drooped and kept his face concealed.

The cell phone in his pocket rang and he answered it. "Hello?"

An unseen hand thrust Leo forward, moving him closer to the image of himself and encouraged him to get close enough to hear the voice on the other end of the telephone.

"I need you to make a drop right now. Three grams on the corner of Stephen and Crag."

Leo recognized the voice. It was Saint Nick.

"All right, I'll be there in twenty minutes," he said and hung up the phone.

"Where do you think you're going? Your father is on his way home and I told you that I'm going to be serving dinner soon."

"I'm going out to take care of some business."

"What have you gotten yourself into?"

Leo ignored her and walked into his dark bedroom. All the shades were drawn and the daylight was successfully blocked out. In the shadows, he watched himself kneel on the floor inside the closet, moving things out of the way and, removing a piece of drywall. Taking a silver box with an embossed image of a fiendish looking imp on the top from the cutout, he opened it. He moved a rubber band roll of money out of the way, grabbed a quarter kilo of prepackaged cocaine, and stuffed it down his pants. Leaving behind another quarter kilo for a drop he was supposed to do later that night, he went to put everything back in the box.

"Leo?" his mother said, approaching the bedroom.

He moved fast and covered the supply with clothing that had been dropped on the floor. He stood and his mother poked her head into his room.

"Be back within the hour, OK?"

"I'll try."

"OK, good. It would be nice to eat as a family."

"Sure, Mom," he said, and pushing past her in the doorway, he exited the house.

Leo stayed behind and watched his mother. She stood at the doorway and seemed to contemplate going inside the room and seeing what he was up to. Instead, she moped down the hallway and sat down at the table and cried. He reached out to touch her, but he didn't know if he should, so he didn't.

Crack!

Leo jumped and so did his mother. She shouted out in fright. The back door had been kicked open and two masked men charged into the house. They rushed his mother and she screamed hysterically. Within two seconds one stifled her voice with a gloved hand that wrapped around her mouth. Her eyes bulged with terror.

"Where is it?" one of the men said.

She tried to speak but the strong grip stifled her voice.

"You scream, you die," the man said and slowly moved his hand away.

"You get away from her," Leo said, and swung at the men. But his efforts were in vain. He was captive, forced to watch a horrible event unfold and he couldn't intervene or look away.

"Your son," one of the men said and took a steak knife from the table. He pressed the tip into her cheek and blood trickled out. "He has something we want. Where is it?"

"I don't know what you're talking about!" The tremble in her voice was heartbreaking.

"You know."

She shook her head and drops of blood dotted her shirt. "I don't."

"She's lying," one of the men said.

"She can deny it all she wants, but she knows," a third man said as he entered the house. He was blurry and Leo couldn't see him. "She'd have to be blind not to know that boy was up to no good."

"You're gonna talk, bitch!" the other man said and slapped her, smearing the blood. He grabbed her hair and dragged her toward the bedrooms in the back of the house.

"Please, why are you doing this?" She kicked and grabbed the wrists that held her hair.

"Because we can," the blurry man said. "This isn't personal, lady—it's business."

The man grabbed her face and squeezed while another held her down. "Which room is his?"

She eyed Leo's bedroom door. "In there."

The man let go of her face and entered Leo's room. Bangs and crashes came from the room as the man conducted a frantic search.

"I've got it," the man said and came out with the silver box, the embossed imp grinning fiendishly as if he relished the chaos and violence. He handed it to the blurry man.

"Please," she said, her voice wrought with fright elevated near a shout.

"Shut yer mouth," the blurry man said, and he knelt in front of her. Opening the box, he showed her the pre-wrapped cocaine and bundle of money that were stuffed inside. "Don't you see what your son has been doing?"

"Oh, Leo," she said and cried.

The blurry man stood and looked at his partners. "Let's go," he said and turned his attention to her. He unsheathed a knife with a white handle. He corrected his grip, wrapping his hand around the handle tightly. "We weren't expecting you to be here. But there can't be any witnesses. It's like I said, nothing personal, it's just business."

"No, don't!" Leo shouted and tried to fend them off. But he wasn't really there.

Three quick jabs with the blurry man's knife to her gut. She whimpered and they let her go. Wheezing, she curled in the fetal position and the men ran out of the house.

Leo moved beside his mother and fell to his knees. Watching her bleed out and fully understanding why he tried to hide from what he had done, he wept.

"Oh, Leo, what have you done?" she muttered.

"I'm sorry, Mom, I didn't mean for this to happen to you."

* * *

Leo jolted awake. His need to erase everything he had just seen from his mind clashed with the reality of what his bad decisions had caused and he was consumed with a toxic mix of guilt and rage. The image on the floor played tricks with his mind and it appeared to move. Eyes filled with blame blinked open and stared at him and hands that came out of the floor shoved him away.

"Go on," he heard his mother say. "Get out of here. Sitting here with this memorial you've designed doesn't help what you did to me. You are the company you keep, Leo. This is your fault. It's time to face that fact."

13

ENTRENCHED

Present Day.

Keir shoved the pointed end of a stick into the soft mud. It had fabric knotted at the top, laced with vine cord, and it burned. As the torch belched a thick gob of smoke into the tunnel, he approached feet that stuck out of a pile of collapsed earth.

"I told you not to come down here, mister," Keir said and grabbed the man by his ankles. He dug his heels deep into the muck and pulled with all of his might. The man moved slightly with each heave, and Keir continued to struggle until the man was clear of the collapse.

"I told you not to come down here," the boy said again. "But you don't ever listen. Now do you believe me that there is no way out of here?"

"Yes," the man said and coughed. His voice was muffled by the confined passageway and he sounded weak and out of breath. "I thought I was dead."

"What you are is a stubborn fool who thinks he knows better. But you don't. You're just a dumb man who only listens to himself."

Keir dragged him out of the narrow passageway and sat next to him, tired.

"I couldn't move and I couldn't breathe," the man said, wiping dirt out of his eyes. He looked like he was wearing a mask. "Thank you for coming and getting me."

"I didn't do it for you. I think you deserve what you got, mister. If it were up to me, I would've left you down here."

"Then why didn't you just let me die?"

"Because you're still needed. Like I said, if it were up to me, I would've done this last part without you, but Twyla is in charge and she thought differently. Lucky for you she thinks this last part needed to play out with you." He slapped the man on the back. "Now let's get out of here before the imp returns."

The man remained unmoved, still trying to catch his breath.

"I don't feel sorry for you, mister. You're the one who didn't want to listen to me and chose to go off on your own. You did this."

"You're right, and it was a foolish move."

"Most of your entire life has been run by foolish moves, mister. You're wallowing in the mud, needing the help of a child. Have you learned humility yet?"

The man looked at the boy, his eyes showing his temper.

"I've gotten you mad?" Keir said and turned away. "Good. Now get on your hands and knees and start crawling because there's nothing good down here."

The man groused as he followed Keir. "Why is it here?"

"What are you talking about, mister?"

"The tunnel, this cabin, the people outside . . . what's this all about?"

"Can't you see? It's about you! They want to show you that you're not in control."

The man shivered.

"You are here now and you belong to the valley," Keir said. "Nothing you do can change that."

The man's hands clapped the wet earth and his knees plowed through the soil, sinking as he shifted his weight from one leg to the other, keeping pace with Keir.

"What do you mean I belong to the valley?" the man said.

"You will be leaving my room soon. The same way you've been bound to my room you will be bound to the forest and the creatures within it."

"Wait, hold on," the man said and stopped.

"There is no holding on, mister," Keir said and kept moving. "We're running out of time and believe me when I tell you that you don't want to face what is digging its way through the other side of that collapse. It is far worse than the imp and the things in the forest."

The man panted. "Are you telling me I'm stuck here forever?"

"That's what I've been telling you since you arrived, mister. But don't worry, you'll get a chance to get back outside."

The man was way behind Keir, whimpering. The boy moved on, his pace steady, the distant beam of light from the hatch ahead.

"Give me a second," the man said.

"I'm showing you mercy by not waiting, mister. I'm telling you to be careful of what lurks in the shadows behind you."

The firelight dimmed the farther Keir moved away from him and the man tasted the darkness again. Not wanting any part of it he crawled fast, slowing only when he caught up to the boy.

"The sad part for you is they haven't even begun to try and get to you yet. They're playing, looking to see how deep your resolve is and they've already cracked you."

"Who?"

"The things in my drawings, mister. Don't you get it?"

"No, I don't get it! What I saw down here looked nothing like the things you drew."

"The imp has nothing to do with the things outside."

"Why was it trying to kill me?"

Keir laughed. "It wasn't trying to kill you mister. It was playing with you."

"Playing?"

"It likes to build your hope and see you crumble when you realize there isn't any. What it got to do with you is its reward for its service to you."

"Why would it do that?"

"Because that's what a trickster likes to do when it's not working."

The man followed Keir in silence for a while before he said, "It is a scary thing."

"As you are to it, mister. It's distrusting and will never allow the person it gets to play with to get too close."

The man shivered and Keir wasn't sure if it was because of the seeping cold or because of his experience with the imp.

"I want you to understand something, mister. No matter how hard you kick my door or how far you crawl into a hole, you can't escape what you must answer for. If you try to resist it, your punishment will only intensify until you learn to comply. Do you get that?"

The man crawled, the hardening ground grinding his hands and knees. "Yeah, I get it."

"Good," Keir said and turned around and looked at the man. "And I'll bet if I asked you to play a game with me now, you wouldn't be so resistant to the idea, would you?"

"No, kid, I wouldn't," the man said, sullen.

"I didn't think so," Keir said as they crawled the rest of the way to the trap door in silence.

14

THE SHELTER

The past.

Welcome

Now Serving

The pain in Leo's belly rolled, making him sweat. Although he didn't think it was from hunger, he hoped the pastor's offering of a meal would help quiet the ache some.

The door to the pantry opened and a stranger made his exit. Leo couldn't help but notice how the man's face looked like an old leather mitt and how his teeth were jagged and discolored. A distinct smell of armpit blasted by him and he wondered what his own smell was like. It had been weeks since he showered, maybe longer. Unless he counted the rain.

He yawned.

The night had been a sleepless one. The confrontation he had with his father, the confusion around seeing his mother lurking in the shadows, and then the disturbing dream about her murder at the hands of the blurry man haunted him.

"The blurry man," he said and looked down the alleyway. Debris swept against the building and standing puddles of water soiled the lane. The window he knocked on the night before was closed tightly, inactivity all around. "It was you, Saint Nick. You're the Blurry Man, you have to be. You killed my mother to get the drugs and money from me that I sold for you. You did it to keep me in debt to you."

But for Leo, there was a measure of doubt that the Blurry Man was indeed Saint Nick.

A second person exited the pantry and held the door for Leo. "Are you going inside?" A strong smell of alcohol surrounded that individual.

Leo snapped out of it and hurried to take the door. He stepped inside and about a dozen people, all male, sat at tables that were separated from each other. Eating ferociously, primitive man was difficult to watch. A few people held trays and stood in line, waiting for an individual in an apron to portion out a meal for them.

"Take a tray next to you and come on up," he was told, the faces around him covered with hair but unable to hide how far they'd fallen and what they had done to their bodies.

He took a tray and stood in line, the arm Saint Nick and his henchmen yanked on hung uselessly at his side, a pulsing reminder of his predicament. A clock on the wall ticked loudly and someone in the room coughed, deep and raspy. Pictures of the pastor hung on the wall, posing with the street people, their names handwritten below the photos.

You need to go back to your father and get the money you owe Saint Nick.

The voice and its demands interrupted him. "He won't give it to me," he whispered, hoping to satisfy it for the time being. "Especially after what I did to him last night."

Then take it from him if you must! Use force tenfold if you need to.

"No," he argued, looking at his feet. "Something isn't right. My dream . . . Saint Nick . . . he has some explaining to do."

"Sir?"

Leo looked up and saw that everyone in front of him had been served.

"Sir?"

Leo followed the voice.

"It's your turn."

Leo looked at a tall young man with a black eye and a scabbed gash across the bridge of his nose.

"Are you hungry?" the young man asked.

Leo looked at the kid's face. Bad acne dotted his cheeks and braces parted his puffy moist lips.

The kid stared back at Leo, frozen in a moment of recognition of someone terrible.

"Something to eat?" the kid managed to say.

Leo placed the tray down and started to walk away.

"It's OK. I'm sure you're hungry," the boy said. "I don't hold a grudge and you need to understand that you're safe here. Please, allow me to serve you something to eat."

Leo stopped and looked at the boy and then had to look away. The damage and pain he'd inflicted on the poor guy because he was desperate for drug money was beyond belief.

"We are glad you came to us and we are happy to help you in your time of need."

Leo resisted his urge to flee and picked up the tray. He walked to the kid and held the tray out.

"I'm sorry," Leo muttered.

"It's OK," he said. "Do you remember my name?"

Leo thought about it and didn't remember. "No, I don't."

"My name is Wendell." He touched his swollen face. "And don't worry about it. It looks worse than it feels. How is yours?"

He was hurting bad but didn't want to say so.

"I, uh . . ."

"What's your name?"

"Leo."

The boy nodded. "I'm glad you stopped by today, Leo." He loaded the plate with a heaping mound of eggs and a side of bacon. "A nice warm meal will help you get through your day."

Pastor Grant walked out of the back and smiled when he saw Leo.

"It's good to see you today."

"Dad," Wendell said. "This is Leo."

Leo looked at the pastor and then at his son. He shrank where he stood, his humiliation deep. The idea that the kid he'd preyed upon and stole from was the son of a pastor, an ambassador of grace, was shameful. It was compounded by the vivid dream of his mother, the interaction he had with his father, and now coming down from his high gave him nothing to hide behind.

"Yes," the pastor said. "I met Leo last night." He extended a hand to Leo and shook it, his knuckles torn.

"They did a number on you last night but I see you tried to fight back. Here," he said and took the tray for Leo. "Come, let's have a seat. We can chat for a while or we can sit together in silence. Either way, I'd like to keep you company."

He followed the pastor and they settled in a corner, away from everyone else. Leo eyed the pictures on the walls. Everyone looked so defeated and lacking love.

"I put them up there so they know they are someone and that someone cares about them."

"Huh?" Leo said, and looked at the pastor.

"Love is important." He slid the tray of food in front of Leo. "Would you like to tell me your story or perhaps something about you that might help me understand you a little better?"

Leo sat back and looked at the pastor. The resemblance from father to son was striking and it conjured a deep sigh. The kindness of the man who sat across from him was something he wasn't used to and he didn't know how to accept it.

"I don't have a story," Leo said plainly.

"Oh, come now, we all have a story to tell. Isn't that what our life is about? They're just stories of struggles and triumphs. But overcoming the struggles is what can help define us and make us stronger."

Truth be told, Leo wasn't sure what his story was. But whatever it might be, he worked really hard to not have to face it.

"That's OK," the pastor said, not allowing the awkward silence to linger too long. "Perhaps if I tell you about myself, maybe it'll allow you to open yourself to me?"

Leo ate.

"Before I turned my life over to serve the Lord, I was living on the streets, desperate to get high, lying, cheating, and stealing and robbing anyone who was unfortunate enough to cross my path."

"What caused you to go out on the streets?" Leo said, his mouth full of food.

"Bad choices, Leo. Plain and simple."

"Did you make those choices or did someone make them for you?"

"They were my own. We are all given free will and a moral compass with which to steer. It's up to you to decide which path to take."

Leo shook his head. "My choices were made for me. There's no such thing as free will."

"Of course there is. God knows every possibility, not what you will choose. You are free to choose love and free to choose sin."

"My parents," he said, and laid his fork down. "They've always been hard on me, expecting me to follow in my father's footsteps. They've always measured success by looking at how fat their wallet is. My mother was a nurse before she had me and my father runs an insane asylum. I swear he brought home a curse from one of his patients and it has been talking to me for years. It tries to tell me what to do and none of it is ever nice. The only way I've learned to silence it is to numb it."

The pastor tapped the table and bounced his knee. "If you put your trust into God, He will help you through this. You need to know that you are under His protection and a curse could not harm you or influence you to do the works of something evil."

"My days of putting my trust into anyone other than myself are over."

"What about the man next door to me?"

Leo could see where the pastor was going and didn't know how to defend himself against it.

"The man that is in the alleyway next to me . . . it seems you've put a lot of trust in him," the pastor said. "I've seen his work and it comes from something evil. Why do you choose to surround yourself with people like him?"

"You should be careful," Leo said. "He's a dangerous man and he doesn't like anyone interfering in his business. I've seen what he can do."

The pastor pointed at Leo's face. "I have, too." The pastor smiled, trying to make light of it. "I'll be OK, Leo. He may have guns and thugs to help his cause, but I have the protection of the Lord. He cannot harm me."

"He'll take your being here as a threat."

"I've been here for two weeks and I'm still OK."

"What about your son?"

The pastor watched his son with a smile before looking back at Leo. "He was attacked by someone desperate in our store the other night. But his sacrifice to the Lord and the people in need of His grace is a worthy one. Profits and donations from the bodega finance these meals."

"The church owns that?"

The pastor smiled. "Who knows, maybe it has fed the person responsible for the attack and it will soften their heart. It's OK, because we forgive those who trespass against us."

Leo fiddled with his fork. "Maybe what happened to your son was a message from Saint Nick?"

"Is that what he calls himself?" The pastor laughed. "Anyway, I go where the Lord guides me and no evil works can knock me from my course."

"I'm sorry someone hurt your son," Leo said. "You're doing a good thing here."

"Thank you. I hope you got something out of our conversation and you come back anytime. When you're ready, I'll take your picture and hang it on my wall because you are important, too. Remember, you have friends here, young man."

The preacher got up and moved to another table and greeted another man dressed in rags with a gentle hand on his shoulder. Leo studied him and he seemed genuine in his cause. Maybe it was as the preacher said. Maybe he did have friends here.

15

THE MAN IN THE MIRROR

Present day.

"I really don't want to go in there," Leo said, and held onto the door jamb with all of his might. The shoulder that hurt screamed out in pain, demanding he let go, but his trepidation of what he stared into prevailed.

"Why, Leo?" Twyla said from the darkness. "What is it about this room that makes you so apprehensive?"

Leo looked at the black veil and could feel it repelling him. It was a sensation of being pushed away by unseen hands and a feeling of its disdain towards him. There was a lingering threat of something bad that was going to happen to him if he dared to cross the barrier.

"Because if I go in there something bad is going to happen to me."

"What would make you say that? It's just a room."

"No, it's not," he said, and noticed that the flicker from the firelight didn't penetrate the black. "There's something ominous about it."

"What do you think is going to happen to you, Leo?"

He searched his feelings and shivered. "I don't know, but I think it's something far worse than the things that are outside."

"There is nothing in here but the truth, Leo," she said, and her hand penetrated the veil. "That's what you're afraid of."

The tremble in her hand prompted Leo to take it just so he could steady it.

"The fire is going to start burning low and there is not much time left before you have to leave here. You need to come and face what you must know about this place and your life because the two are intertwined."

With a gentle tug from Twyla, he was pulled into the darkness. To his amazement, the room was well lit and what he saw took his breath away.

Beyond the room he now stood in and straight ahead was a hallway with a high arched ceiling. Thick wooden beams crisscrossed and a cobblestone floor was lit by iron sconces mounted on the walls. On both sides of the hallway were bookcases that went from the floor to the ceiling. Stocked on the shelves were countless leather bound books that stretched on and disappeared into the far distance.

"What is this?" he said, and what he saw lured him further into the room.

Twyla slipped the book he'd tried to burn into a snug spot on the wall.

"This is the library of the dead, Leo."

"The what?" He swallowed hard and his eyes went wide. His jaw dangled open as he looked from the long hallway back at Twyla.

"These books," Twyla said. "They contain stories about everyone who has or is going to arrive here in the valley. These hallways of books run underground and are interconnected with all of the cabins so their keepers can understand and prepare for their visitors."

"Keepers?" Leo said, the word mumbled, his mind trying to comprehend.

"What was that?" Twyla said.

"Keepers like you and Keir?"

She nodded. "Servants to the dead. Our appearance is merely symbolic of the two most important stages of life. You see, Keir represents youth—the beginning of life. I represent the elderly or people nearing the end of their lives. And everything in between is what you've wasted in your life."

"I don't understand."

"You were given a gift and you decided you no longer wanted it. Can you think of a reason why?"

"I don't know of any gift," Leo said and looked around. The ominous firelight from the sconces singed the brick walls and cast shadows that took the shapes of faces that were in pain, projecting them on the walls, floor, and ceiling. He didn't want to see them so he closed his eyes and squeezed them tightly.

"And what about the darkness?" he said.

"What about it?"

He opened his eyes and the images were gone. "Why couldn't I see inside this room from in there?" He pointed at the veil that separated the two rooms.

"Because the darkness is your light. You needed to step past the threshold to understand that."

"What do you mean?"

"The light inside you is gone forever, Leo. The darkness is where you sought comfort and it has overtaken you and it now defines you."

"It has overtaken me?" he said, his words falling at his feet and his focus on the endless row of books. He rubbed his hands together, nervous. "There are so many . . ."

He licked his lips and watched Twyla shuffle towards him.

"How many people are in those books?" he said.

"More than I can count, and sadly, everyone that is supposed to be. They're all as lost as you."

"How did they get there? I mean, why would Sariel put them in there?"

"Sin," Twyla said. "Everything you see here is because of sin. It carries a heavy price."

A winged creature fluttered around in the distance, moving from shelf to shelf searching for something. It pulled a book out of the shelf and immediately returned it. Moving to a different location, it searched some more and distracted Leo from what Twyla was telling him.

"What is that thing?" he said and continued to watch it with growing interest. It hovered in front of a shelf and chose a book. The weight of it made the thing dip in flight but it quickly recovered. It flipped through the pages while its wings worked hard to keep it afloat.

"Come," Twyla said and took his hand again and led him to a tree stump in the middle of the room. "This is a lot for you to take in and I think it best you sit."

Leo sat and watched the flying thing with fire-red skin. It carried the book away far into the distance and Leo observed it until he lost sight of it.

"What is it doing?"

"Delivering a book to a cabin of keepers. Someone new is about to arrive and the keeper must come up with a plan to reveal that person's past and set them off on their new path."

"I don't like the sound of that," Leo said and realized it was a good thing Twyla had him sit. The discovery of the library and its infinite literature, seeing the flying creature, and coming to terms with what these cabins functioned as left him both speechless and dizzy.

"You don't need to say anything. If you give me a moment, it will become clear," she said and walked to what appeared to be a tree growing out of the wall in a shadowy corner, hidden from the firelight that illuminated the library of the dead.

Twyla lit a match and began igniting candles that sat at the tips of the branches. The wall of the room beside the tree came to life and Leo looked at his reflection cast from a giant mirror that took up the entire wall.

"Now you will come to know why you are here," Twyla said. "To do this, you must tell me what you see."

He stood up and moved close to the mirror. His face looked like he was wearing a bone mask and his eyes were tired and encased with dark rings that spoke of poor health and lack of sleep. His body looked frail and weak and he didn't like to look at what he'd become. He closed his eyes and bowed his head.

"What happened to me?"

"I know what you see is difficult to face. You've been sick for a long time now. You've been poisoning your body for the better part of a year. And the saddest part is the people closest to you are the ones that have suffered the most. You've deceived them, stolen from them, and left them broken."

She extinguished the match and positioned herself behind him. The tree of life burned bright, revealing everything about him, leaving no question about what he saw.

"Look at me," she said.

He looked at her in the reflection of the mirror and she was beautiful. Turning around, she looked old and tired again.

"I think I'd like to offer you a chance to confront the person who is most responsible for your misfortune."

He remained still, continuing to stare at her, confused by what he saw in the reflection of the mirror.

"You would like a chance to do that, wouldn't you?"

"What?" Leo said, his focus drifting.

"Do you want to confront the person responsible for your privation?"

"Yes," he said and looked at himself again in the mirror. He hated what he saw and the things she was telling him. The way the mirror was tricking him. Why did it make him look so bad but make her something other than what he saw with his own eyes?

She walked away. "Then sit."

He sat and she placed her hands on his shoulders, continuing to look at him through the reflection of the mirror. "You are starting to see things for the way they are now."

"But you look different in the mirror."

"Indeed I do, because you are seeing what's inside."

"Inside?"

She patted her chest over her heart. "Suppose I told you the person responsible for what you see was behind that mirror, watching you right now? What is it you would like to tell him?"

"That I was pissed off," Leo said, looking over his shoulder at Twyla.

"Don't tell me," Twyla said. "Tell him." She pointed at the mirror. "He is behind that glass right now and you need to tell him how you feel."

Leo looked at his reflection; the anger that looked back at him was dangerous and pervasive. "What did you do to me?"

"What does it look like he's done?"

"He's ruined my life!"

"And the people closest to you," she said.

"Who is behind that mirror? Is it the guy Keir took in? Is that who is back there?"

"Yes," Twyla said, her response calm. "It is him."

"I can't believe I was concerned about him, that I even begged you to let him inside. I did that and he did this to me?"

Twyla smiled. "I need you to control your rage. Before you can confront the man behind the mirror, you first need to understand the one you can see looking back at you. And to do that I need to show you who you were in life so you can confront what you are in death," Twyla said.

"What I am in death?" Leo said and looked at her, perplexed.

"Yes Leo. You are here, in this valley, inside my cabin, seeing the library of the dead because you have been named in the book."

16

CONFRONTING SIN

The past.

Leo stood across the street from his parents' house, hidden behind a thick oak tree. He'd been watching the house for any signs of his mother, haunted by the details of his dream and his inability to separate his world of fantasy and what was real.

She's not in there.

"I don't believe you," he said, watching through a window with an open shade as his father talked to another man.

Then go up there and knock on the door. See if she answers.

A police car sat in the driveway. It had been there since he arrived.

"I can't do that. Especially after what I did yesterday."

Well you can't stand out here all day. Your mother isn't there.

"How do you know for sure?"

Because that's what we worked so hard to keep you from remembering.

"No," he said and his knees buckled. The moisture in the grass and soil seeped into the knees of his pants. "It can't be true."

It is.

"What of my dream?"

The voice inside went quiet and the pastor's words weighed heavily on him. There was so much he wanted to say to his parents but he knew he would never get that chance. But even if he did get that opportunity, he wouldn't know where to start. The truth was the furthest thing away from him.

And you wouldn't mean it.

"You're right. Because there's something wrong with me. I made that up about the curse because it annoyed my father. What happened to that man is something that has haunted him for a long time. If I was going to suffer, so was he."

He won't get sympathy from me.

"I can't believe I knocked my father down so I could take from him."

You didn't have a choice.

"Yes I did! Didn't you hear what the preacher said?"

Who cares about the preacher and what he has to say?

"I do."

Yeah, but for how long?

"Screw you!"

The same way Saint Nick did to you and your mom?

Leo stood and began to walk away. The voice was the last thing he wanted to hear.

Where are you going? To lay with that pathetic thing you scratched into the ground?

"Shut up."

No one wants you, Leo, not even me.

"Leave me alone," Leo growled, loathing everything—even the encouraging words Pastor Grant gave him.

You've kept me waiting and I don't like it. If you get me what I need, I'll leave you alone.

* * *

Leo ran down the alley and pounded on the window with the heavy drawn shade.

"I know you're in there!" he shouted, and the echo of his voice caused a neighborhood dog to bark.

He pounded the window again and the glass rattled inside the frame.

"Tell Nick I want him out here now!"

Running behind the building and to the small missing window, he tossed rocks inside.

"Come on, get yer ass out here!"

"Leo!" Saint Nick said and came out a rear entrance Leo hadn't noticed before. Dressed properly in his red suit, his face was as bright as the fabric—and two of his henchmen were beside him. "What the hell do you think you're doing?"

"I've come to pay my debt," he said.

"This is how you come?"

He walked towards Leo and the click of Nick's expensive shoes on the cement made him tense.

"Are you tweaking or something?"

"No," Leo said, soaking with sweat. Nothing about the moment felt real. "I don't know, maybe."

"This is how you come to my place of business?"

"I . . ."

"You break the veil of secrecy and act the fool?"

Leo's anger settled into humility. He placed himself in this situation without thinking things through and didn't know how he was going to get himself out of it.

Saint Nick nudged one of his men and they went to Leo, pushed him up against the wall, and searched his pockets. "He's got nothing on him boss."

"You said you came to pay your debt and yet you come with nothing? Did you come here to die, Leo, is that your plan?"

"I'm not sure," he said.

"Have you given up on your life?"

In a moment of clarity, he remembered his mother, his father, the pastor, and his dream. "I've come to tell you that my debt to you has been paid. I'm done."

"Oh?" Saint Nick said, and he was close now, appraising Leo.

"I have a drawing in my room. It's on my floor and it's of a person in the fetal position."

"What does that have to do with the money you owe me?"

"I've been avoiding it for a long time and I've come to you to help me forget the pain of that. The thing is, I never looked at what was staring me right in the face the whole time."

Saint Nick crossed his arms. "Oh yeah, what's that?"

"That the death of that person, although I was shouldering the responsibility of the tragedy . . . I've come to realize you and your men are the ones who came into my house and took my stash. They took the money, too, and then you killed my mother because none of you counted on her being home."

Saint Nick laughed and his men mimicked him. "That's absurd, Leo. The shit you're on has turned your brain into mush."

"Has it?"

Leo felt like a gazelle staring into the face of a lion.

"Hmm," Saint Nick said and ran his fingers over the fabric of the suit, smoothing it out. "I suppose that might make sense to someone as screwed up as you. But I didn't do that."

Leo stepped forward, correcting his posture. "You did. You called me so I would go and make a drop. You knew it would get me out of the house and give you more than enough time to get the money and the drugs."

"Don't blow up on me, Leo," Saint Nick said and one of the men lunged at Leo, hitting him in the gut. Leo fell to a knee and gasped for air. "You don't come into my house and speak to me like that and expect to get away with it. You don't accuse me, and you certainly don't disrespect me."

Leo struggled to his feet, holding his stomach.

"Yes, I called you to make a drop," Saint Nick said. "I did it so you could earn your keep. What I give you costs money."

"You've never given anyone anything. Saint Nick . . ." he laughed. "That's a joke. You've never given anyone anything for free."

Saint Nick nodded at his man and he hit Leo again in the same spot. This time Leo fell down on all fours.

"There, I just gave you that free of charge."

Leo crawled around and tried to catch his breath. His chest burned and his eyes watered.

"So don't you ever say I've never given you something for free."

Saint Nick began to circle him like a hunter sizing up his prey.

"You should be careful what you're accusing me of, Leo," Saint Nick said. "You're making me sound like a thief and a thug instead of a businessman."

"I'm just telling you how things look to me," Leo said.

"You're a junkie, Leo. Nothing around you makes any sense." He squatted in front of Leo. "You've become paranoid and think everything is a conspiracy."

Saint Nick lashed out and grabbed Leo's hair and his henchmen held his hands behind his back, forcing him to his feet. Saint Nick grabbed his chin and centered his focus. "There's no coming back from what you are and the line you just crossed with me. I've done all I can for you, but I think we'd all be better off if you joined your momma."

Those words were as close to a confession Leo would ever get from Saint Nick and they sparked his anger. He struggled against the hands that held him, growling deep in his throat as he tried to get at Saint Nick. But Saint Nick laughed and stabbed Leo in the stomach, twisting the knife.

17

SOMETHING HIDDEN

Present Day.

Keir closed the hatch with a heavy thump and groaned as he struggled to push the toy box over the trapdoor.

"That's OK, mister," he grunted. "Don't worry about helping me. I've got it."

The man shivered in the middle of the room, his arms crossed, dirt falling onto the floor, his focus still deep inside that hole and on the thing that tricked him.

"People can be so hard headed but I can't say that I'm surprised about what you did. If I've seen one, I've seen a thousand just like you," Keir said, and sat on the box and rested. "Why you chose to go into that hole instead of playing a game is a mystery to me."

"I wanted to get out of here," the man said. His teeth chattered and his eyes remained firmly on the toy box.

"Since you arrived, all you've wanted to do is get out of here. I find it odd how little thought you put into why you're here or how you got here in the first place."

"I've been in strange places before and have found my way out. But never a place quite like this."

"You're going to have to forget what happened in that hole because what's about to happen is going to be a whole lot worse."

"How can it get any worse than that?"

The man's eyes were wide with the question and Keir shrugged.

"You'll see," Keir said and handed the man his jacket. "Put it on so you can warm up."

The man did but still stared at the toy box. Something made a bumping sound in that corner and the candlelight flickered.

"What was that?" the man said.

"It wasn't anything more than the creak and groan of an old cabin settling."

"No," he said, and pointed at the hatch. "That sound came from in there. The thing you said was coming for me, the one that was digging out the collapse, can it get in here? Is that why you said it's going to get worse?"

Keir laughed. "No, mister, that's not it at all. You're funny."

"There's nothing funny about this, kid."

"Well, this side of you is a whole lot better than dealing with the belligerent and arrogant side."

"How can you blame me for wanting to get out of here?"

"I don't blame you for wanting to get out of here, mister, I'm blaming you for the way you are. It seems the imp has really put the fear in you. Humbled you some."

The man moved to the table and sat. Sweat glistened on his forehead and he shivered. "Maybe we can play that game you were wanting to play with me before?"

Keir shook his head. "We can't, mister. You and your tantrums have used up all of our time together. Any chance we had to play is over."

"How can you say the time for play is over?" He looked around the room, confused. "We're locked inside here and you said we couldn't get out and whatever is in that tunnel can't get in. So come on—" he patted the tabletop—"sit and let's play."

Keir walked around the room and picked up the jacks that were still scattered across the floor. He dropped them in the brown paper bag. "This is why Twyla gets so frustrated with people like you. You don't seek to understand until it's too late. Time has run out, mister."

"Here, let me help you," the man said and stood. He bent to pick up a jack between his feet but his cold fingers wouldn't close around the small metal object.

"I've got it," Keir said and swiped the jack. He folded the bag and put it away.

The man stood in the center of the room, flexing his hand. "I can't feel anything."

"You've always been like that."

"What?"

"Cold. Lacking in feelings. Your life was a perversion, mister. Why would you be so desperate to get back to that?"

"Because it was good to me."

"So, Twyla and I were right about you. You are a broken man."

"We can sit at that table of yours right there and talk. You can tell me everything I need to know and you can help me fix this."

Keir shook his head. "You should have listened to me when I first asked you to talk with me. At least you would have gained some insight as to why you've got to go into the judgment room now."

"Oh, OK," the man said and even laughed. "Is this a game you want to play?"

"It's not a game, mister," Keir said and pushed on a wooden knot engrained in the wall above the toy box. Something clicked and hissed and then the wall moved, exposing a seam that was invisible only moments ago. It looked like a doorway to a hidden passage.

Keir grabbed the lip and gave it a tug. Without sound, a door swung open and revealed a small dark room with a single seat that faced a blank wall.

"I'm going to need you to go in there, mister."

The man hesitated and then nodded. "Yeah, sure, I'll go along with it. Just tell me what I have to do."

"Go in there and have a seat."

"And then what?"

"I close the door behind you and then you wait and see."

"Can we do something else, maybe?" The man looked at the room. "Dark places aren't where I want to be right now."

"No, you've got to go in there! Our time together is almost over."

"I'm not going in there, kid, I can't. You can't expect me to do that. Especially after what I just went through."

"I do, because if you would have listened to me when you first arrived, I was going to explain that this room is a prep room—an attempt to get you ready for the judgment room. And that—" he pointed at the small hidden room—"is the judgment room. But, instead, you chose to go off on some crazy adventure. I'm sorry you are the way you are, but you need to get in there."

"No," the man said and hurried to the door he arrived through. Grabbing the handle, he gave it a strong, desperate tug and to his surprise, it didn't resist him. He opened it a crack.

"No, mister, don't do that," Keir said and pushed the door shut.

"It's open."

"Yes, it's open. You still haven't listened to me," Keir said. "And I'm warning you not to open this door, mister!"

"Get out of my way, kid, and let me get the hell outta here."

"You won't like what's waiting for you out there."

"I don't like what might be waiting for me in there either." He pointed at the small room. "That thing in your cellar, hidden doors in the wall, your creepy drawings, it's all too much."

Keir unwrinkled a piece of paper soiled with dirt and handed it to the man. "What's behind this door isn't a kind old woman mister."

The man looked at the paper and tossed it aside. It was the drawing Keir had made of that deformed creature. The same one the man had pulled off the wall earlier, wiped his shoes with, and crumpled in a ball and tossed on the floor. "What are you giving me that for?"

"I told you they don't like being discarded like they're pieces of trash, mister. I'm telling you that you need to face what is waiting for you in that other room. If you open this door, the thing on that paper might be out there, looking to get its hands on you so you pay for disgracing him."

The man wrestled with Keir's warning. "I have to trust my instincts," he said and placed his foot behind the door and pulled it open a crack, hoping to spy what was outside the door. To his surprise, a crying eye looked back at him. It was a woman and the sadness he saw took away his worry.

"Don't open that door, mister!"

He opened the door a little more and said, "Are you OK?"

A middle-aged woman with messy hair and wild eyes rammed the door and knocked him backwards. She charged into the room and shrieked, "Look at what you did to me!"

The man backpedaled into the room, his eyes wide with terror, his arms raised as they tried to fend off untamed punches that seemed to come from every direction. The door slammed shut behind the woman.

"I didn't do anything to you!"

The woman stopped, pointed at the man, and broke out in a fit of laughter. "You are such a liar!" She stomped her feet as she approached him. Blood soaked her shirt and pants and dripped onto the floor. "How can you deny doing this to me?" She withdrew an ivory handled knife that stuck out of her abdomen. She raised the blood-coated weapon over her head. "I should kill you for what you did to me!" She charged after him a second time, but he ran for the judgment room and pulled the door shut.

The man heard the woman bang into the door and stab at the wood.

"I'll kill you for what you've done!" she said, her voice easy to hear through the thin wall.

"Missus?" The man could hear Keir say. The man tried to quiet his thundering heart so he could listen to what was being said.

The woman whimpered and the distinct sound of the knife clattering across the floor could be heard, followed by sobbing.

"It's OK," Keir said.

"No, it's not OK," the woman said. "How could someone not remember doing that to another human being?"

"It is time for you to leave here," Keir said. "Take closure knowing he's going to face his judgment for what he's done to you and everyone else."

The man listened to the footsteps fading and heard the door bang shut. Everything went silent. Surrounded by a darkness so black he couldn't see an inch in front of his face, he reached his hand out and touched the smooth, cool surface of the wall in front of him and gave in to the tremble in his limbs.

Sitting, he exhaled hard. But before he could settle, a dim light began to shine on the other side of the wall.

He could see candles burning in a tree, revealing a man and an old woman talking. He couldn't hear what was being said but the man he watched stared at him with a hatred so deep, he shifted uncomfortably. Searching the hidden door for a handle or trip lever, he couldn't find anything.

He looked back at the man; the way he stared was fierce and left him with the impression that they were gathered because of him and that the wrath of that anger would be heading his way soon.

18

A CONFRONTATION

Present day.

"He did those things?" Leo said and watched Twyla in the mirror. She stood behind him and her eyes appeared as stones of disappointment in the moody light.

"Is that all you can remember?" she said, hovering over him like an interrogator.

"Yes." He shivered. "He did that to me and my mother," he said and pointed at the mirror. "And he shouldn't be allowed to get away with it."

Twyla folded her arms across her chest. "I couldn't agree with you more. And trust me, he won't."

Leo stood up and moved close to the mirror, his breath fogging the glass as he tried to see the man behind the reflection. But his own face, contorted by discontent of himself and the actions of someone else was the only thing he could see and he slapped the glass.

"I hate him for what he's done to me!" He turned away, fists clenched and his face packed with rage.

"I want you to tell him," Twyla said. "Tell him how you feel right now and don't hold back."

"I feel violated," he said in a deep whisper, his face folding into something that looked similar to the things outside. He turned and faced the mirror, his fists pumping stiffly at his sides, the veins bulging in his neck. "I hate you, do you hear me? It wasn't bad enough you ruined my life, but you had to include my mother in this?"

He opened his hands and flexed them. Kneeling, he lowered his voice and stared in the mirror. "If I get my hands on you I'm going to kill you for what you did."

He sat in silence. The idea that the man who encouraged his addiction and manipulated him was behind that glass, safe, made him seethe.

"What are you hoping to do next, Leo?"

He stood and his ominous reflection and the flickering light mimicked his mood perfectly. Dark, pulsing, and eerie, Twyla was right, he had become one with the shadows.

"I want to tell him how I feel to his face. I need to see his fear as he's seen mine and my mother's. I am going to turn the predator into the prey."

"Very well," Twyla said as if his fury was the natural place for him. She went to the tree and had difficulty blowing out the candles.

When the mirrored wall went dark, she started her slow walk back to the main room of the cabin and Leo followed, his focus on all the things he wanted to do.

"Leo?" she said and stopped at the threshold, out of breath from trying to extinguish the flames.

He looked at her and could see her lips upturned at the corners of her mouth. What he was about to do to the man on the other side of that wall was anything but funny.

"You need to know he's been watching you and knows you're coming. Ready yourself for the unexpected."

"Good," Leo said.

She chuckled and carried on, walking into the main room, down the hallway, and to Keir's closed door.

19

OBSERVATION

Present day.

The person on the on the other side of the glass shouted but his words went unheard. He approached the glass and sat, speaking at times in what appeared to be a calmer voice. The man in the red suit worked hard to try and read his lips but came away with nothing. The only thing that was clear to him was that this man on the other side of the glass was angry about something and he was sure it had to do with him.

"Hey!" he said and pounded on the glass. "I'm in here, come and tell me what you're saying so I can hear you."

But the other guy didn't react and the man gave up trying to get his attention. He sat with him, using the silence to study him. Touching the glass in recognition of the angry man, he had a connection with him he couldn't piece together.

"But if they won't let you over here I'll try and listen," the man said and waited.

The old woman said something to the angry man and he stood. The man stood, too, watching them, trying to see something that would help him understand what they were talking about and why he seemed to be so angry.

But it was no use. The glass wall was too thick and it was apparent that it was designed so the people on the other side couldn't see or hear whoever was in this room.

The two spoke some more and the angry man pointed at the glass.

"Me?" the man said and pointed at himself. "You are talking about me, aren't you?"

The old woman struggled to blow out the candles, and with that, the wall in front of him dimmed and went black, leaving him in darkness.

"What is this about?" he said, his voice dull in the small room that felt even smaller now that the darkness encompassed him. He waited with a nervous tremble at what was to come next.

And as if in response, the door that locked him in the room opened and Keir was there, waiting. No smile, no words to help him through this moment. He was just there.

"What is going on?" the man said.

"It's time you face the man who was on the other side of that glass, mister."

"I don't even know who he is."

"Yes you do," Keir said and stepped to the side, allowing him passage.

"Who is he?"

"Someone you've had a profound effect on. Now come."

"I don't want to."

"You must. He's going to be at that door any moment now and you must be ready."

"Ready for what?"

The boy laughed. "Get ready to face the truth and fight for your life. It is the only thing left for you to do here, mister."

"But I haven't learned anything."

"You've learned all that you need. Now stand over here, and when that door opens, you need to step outside right away so that you can confront him before he gets to you."

Somberly, the man exited the secret room and stood where Keir had instructed him. He shifted from foot to foot, nervous, and he rolled up his sleeves.

Keir closed the secret door and stood next to the man. Looking up at him, he said, "Goodbye, mister."

20

WHO IS THERE

Present day.

Leo pounded on Keir's door.

"It's unlocked," Twyla said, standing behind him. "You can go inside whenever you're ready."

"Saint Nick," Leo growled and opened the door with a furious push. The door flung open and a gust of air rushed out of the room and collided with him. Staggering backwards as if he'd been hit by a punch, he shook his head to try and dislodge the dizzying feeling.

"What's wrong?" Twyla said and tried to help him.

"I don't know," he said and leaned against the wall. "I feel lightheaded." He went down to a knee. "Did something just hit me?"

"Don't be silly. Can you stand?"

"Give me a second. My heart is pounding and I'm confused. When I opened the door it felt like something shoved me."

"That's more accurate than saying you were hit. Come," she said and helped him get steady on his feet. She guided him to the door. "Don't forget why you came here."

Leo entered the room and Keir sat at a table. He was drawing faces on paper with crayon and Leo could see that they resembled the things outside perfectly.

"Where is he?" Leo said.

"Where is who, mister?"

The boy placed his crayon down.

"The man you brought in here. The one you and Twyla worked so hard to keep from me."

Keir looked at Twyla and stood.

"He's inside you, mister," Keir said. "You were rejoined the moment you opened that door."

Leo looked at Twyla. "What is he talking about?"

"I've got to sit," Twyla said and moved to the table and sat. She grunted. "My back and feet are killing me and getting you to this moment has been a difficult process."

"Don't act confused, mister. What I said was clear and left no room for question. The man who was inside here with me is inside you," Keir said.

"What are you talking about? I'm not Saint Nick."

"No, you're not," Twyla said.

"So where is he?" Leo said, his eyes volleying between Twyla and Keir.

"He's alive and well right now," Keir said. "He's still doing business in that alley."

"But you told me to talk to the man behind the mirror," Leo said. "You made it seem like Saint Nick was behind it."

"I made no such assumption. You came to that conclusion on your own."

"Don't you understand, mister? It was your own reflection you were talking to," Keir said.

"You've been telling yourself lies for so long that what you recounted of the events was your truth. Not the truth."

"Everything you claimed to have happened was all really just lies," Keir said.

"What are you talking about? I saw you bring a man into the cabin from outside! I heard him banging on the door and he was fearful of the things outside just like I was."

"He was a part of you," Twyla said. "He was a thing you made up in your mind because you envied him. His power, fancy clothes, and money were all the things you thought were glamorous about him."

Leo looked around the room and the walls were bare, the floor clean and neat. There was no sign of anyone else having been in the room but Keir and his things at the table.

"The room behind the mirror, where is it?"

"Go ahead and show him," Twyla said to Keir.

The boy nodded and turned on his heels. He pushed on the knot above the toy box and the wall shifted. He pulled on the lip, exposing the small empty room.

"It is as Keir said. You were joined back together when you opened the door," Twyla said. "You felt that and said so. Besides, I saw it with my own eyes."

"This is crazy," Leo said and chuckled. He stuffed his hands into his pockets.

"What did you expect to find in here, Leo?"

He crossed his arms then put his hands back into his pockets. "You already know the answer to that question."

"Well, I need you to tell me."

"Saint Nick."

"Why do you think he would be here with you?"

"Because he's the one that got me hooked on drugs and he killed my mother."

Twyla shook her head and Leo looked at Keir. The boy didn't attempt to hide his disappointment.

"Why are you shaking your head at me?" Leo said.

"You have it all wrong," Twyla said.

"You're the person responsible for your sins, mister," Keir said. "What you thought were the actions of someone else were really your own."

"He gave me drugs!"

"You took them, Leo, by your own free will," Twyla said. "And because of that you descended into a deep dark hole. It was so deep you had little chance to climb out of it, and the help you were given came in many forms, but you chose not to accept it—at least not until it was too late. You destroyed your life and the lives of the people around you and you're responsible for that."

"You've sinned," Keir said. "And you tried to cover it up and build your own truth to try and hide from it. You can't hide from the things you've done."

"You have to face what really happened," Twyla said. "And accept your punishment."

"Saint Nick did this to me!" he shouted.

"The truth is often scary and sometimes hard to face, mister," Keir said. "Your story is a tragic one indeed and you're seeing the difficulty in accepting that truth."

"How am I supposed to accept a truth that I don't even know about? I've been manipulated since I got here and have been told things that are impossible."

"Then perhaps it is time for you to see what you've really done?"

"You're not going to like what you see, mister. And it's not going to make you feel any better about yourself."

21

WHAT HE REALLY DID

The past

"What?" Leo shouted at his closed door, roused by a barrage of thumps.

"Come on, Leo, open the door," his mother said and knocked again but this time with more force.

"Go away. I'm sleeping," he said and tossed to his side and pulled the blankets over his head. He didn't feel well.

"I'm not going away," she said and tried the handle. "Unlock the door, Leo. You've slept the entire day away and I told you two hours ago that I wanted to talk to you before your father got home from work."

Leo kicked his blankets aside and got up with a huff. His balance was off but his frustration drove him. Grabbing his sweatshirt and pulling the hood over his head, he opened the door a pinch. "I'm tired of hearing your lectures, Mom, and I could care less about what Dad has to say. I don't feel well. Now go away and leave me alone."

"You don't feel well because you've been out partying again. Your father and I are done putting up with your nonsense, Leo. We've given you a chance to make a change, but you're either unwilling or incapable to do so on your own. So now we're going to make you make a change."

"Is that what this is about?" he said and laughed. "Change? Really?"

They stared at each other, neither one budging.

"Stop waking me up for stupid crap like this," he said and pushed the door closed. He approached his bed. "We've been through this a million times already. I'm tired of you guys telling me what to do."

His mother opened the door and the light from the hallway flooded his room, hurting his eyes.

"Get out of my room," he said. "I'm not kidding. That's why I lock the door, because you think you can come in whenever you want."

"You're untrustworthy, Leo, and I can come in whenever I want."

"No you can't!"

"We work and pay the bills. You don't do anything but party and sleep the day away."

"So what!"

"So what?"

"Yeah, I said so what. I'm not hurting anyone."

His mother went to say something but stopped. Her eyes welled with tears and her lips quivered.

"I don't want the tears, Mom. This is getting so old."

"If you could see how much you've changed in the past six months, you'd know why I'm so sad."

"Boohoo," he said, and lay in bed. "It's my life and I'll do whatever I want. Close the door on your way out. I told you I'm not feeling well and the light is bothering my eyes."

"I don't care how you feel," his mother said and stormed into the room. She pulled the shades off the windows and broke them. The afternoon sunlight flooded the messy room revealing half eaten meals, piles of dirty clothes, and open dresser drawers that had been stripped bare.

"What the hell are you doing?"

She looked around the room in disgust. "How do you live like this, Leo?"

He jumped out of bed and shoved his mother. "Get the hell out of my room!"

His mother backpedaled, tripped, and bounced off the wall. She righted herself and an expression of anger contorted her face. "Don't you dare put your hands on me. You'll need to pack a bag because when your father comes home from work, we're taking you to a rehab facility and we're going to clean up this filth."

"I'm not going anywhere and don't touch my things."

"You are going, Leo. You can't live like this any longer," she said and walked to the door. "You either go or you're out of this house. You've lied to us, stolen from us, and now you're getting physical. I'm done and I know your father is done, too. You have about an hour before he gets home. I suggest you start packing your bags and come to terms with it quickly because either way you're leaving this house today."

Leo watched her walk away. He sat on the edge of his bed and tried to wrap his head around everything that just happened and the things she just said.

He hadn't seen her this mad or determined before and until he could figure out what he needed to do, he figured it best that he went along with it. Besides, he was a bit disoriented from being awoken so abruptly. Leo took the silver box and placed it in a duffle bag, tossed in a pair of rumpled up pants and zipped it closed. His mind continued to work on his mother's words but all he could do was hear the bitterness in her tone.

"She's crazy if she thinks I'm going anywhere."

He hated the fact that she thought she could just barge into his room and jump all over his case. Why didn't she just leave him alone?

Shouldering the bag, he went into the kitchen to find his mother but she wasn't there. Still without a plan in mind, he mindlessly took a knife out of the holder and tucked it up his sleeve.

Making his way around the house, he moved in accidental silence. The tick of the grandfather clock pinged like a silent scream; the whir of the air conditioning pushing air around the house shushed like a chant from a whispering chorus saying his name, encouraging him to do something; and the finger-tapping sound of a keyboard was like an encrypted code calling him over.

His mother was at the computer, typing away, chatting with someone in one of those stupid public bingo game rooms. He looked over her shoulder and read what she was typing.

I hate having 2 do this 2 him but he has 2 go.

His fingers curled around the knife handle and he picked out a spot on the side of her neck. If he were to slice her there she would live for a little while and he would be able to see her surprise. That's what she deserved because no matter how hard he tried he couldn't understand how a mother could be so cruel to her own child. She just discarded him like he was worthless.

"Mom?" Leo said and she gasped and turned in her chair.

"Oh, Leo, you scared me," she said, her shaking hand over her heart. "I didn't hear you come up behind me."

His grip loosened on the knife as he saw the sadness in her face. She was crying. "I'm sorry, Mom."

She looked at the bag over his shoulder and smiled. "You've decided you're going to go to the rehab center?"

"You put it in a way like I didn't have a choice. Do I?"

She shook he head. "You're sick, Leo, and you need help. I'm sorry it has come to this." She stood. "We're only doing this because we love you."

She hugged him and he resisted it at first. His duffle bag slipped off his shoulder and rested somewhere by his feet.

"I love you, son."

He hugged her back, distant, not believing a word she said.

"Then why are you trying to send me away?"

"We're trying to help you, Leo. You're twenty-five years old and have to get your life together. The partying has to stop."

"It doesn't feel like you're trying to help me," he said and took the knife and gently pushed it into her stomach and pulled it upwards. Her grip loosened and he stepped back and watched her face. Her expression was frozen, captured somewhere between shock and pain.

"That's what it feels like you're doing to me," he said, surprised the gut was so hard to cut into.

"Why?" she gasped, her eyes as big as quarters.

"Yes, Mom, why?" he said and she fell forward, her body weight pressing the knife in even deeper. He stepped back and withdrew the knife and she fell to the floor.

"Why have you forsaken your only son?"

She rolled around before she slowly shrank into the fetal position, gurgling on blood that spilled from her mouth.

Leo lay on the floor next to her, looking into her glazing eyes, her mouth agape and drawing quick, shallow breaths. He reached out and touched his hand to hers, rubbing gently.

"It's OK to let go, Mom. I want you to die."

And with those words, he stood and picked up his duffle bag. Walking through the house, he knocked things over. His phone rang and it was Saint Nick.

"Hello?" he said, and listened to the instructions he was being given. "OK, I'll be there in a half hour."

He hung up the phone, took a fake flower out of a vase, and looked at his mother one last time. She continued to gasp for air, her breathing shallow, and a horrible bubbling sound filled her throat. He dropped the flower next to her.

"Now I'm going to get wasted and try and forget this ever happened."

Exiting the house, he was satisfied it looked like a robbery gone bad and that he had a strong alibi.

22

THE VALLEY

Present day.

Twyla exited Keir's room and Leo followed her; the accusation made against him was outrageous.

"I didn't do these things you're telling me," he said. "It was Saint Nick. I could never do that to my own mother."

"You did it, Leo, and you tried to hide your guilt and remorse within your drug abuse."

"It can't be. I'm sure I'd have some recollection about something like that."

"You used drugs most of your young adult life and it only intensified after you did this to your mother. Day after day, you did everything you could to escape this reality," Twyla said.

"You people are insane thinking I would kill my own mother. What motive would I have to do that?"

"To keep using. That's what drug abusers do," Twyla said and approached him. She lifted his shirt. "This," she said, referring to the cut on his stomach. "And this." She touched his tender shoulder and pointed at his head. "They are all related to the injuries you sustained before you died. You've carried them over with you."

"I'm not dead! This is some sort of joke . . . or maybe it's a bad high."

"Yea, though I walk through the valley of the shadow of death," Twyla said.

"Do you know that prayer, mister?" Keir said.

Leo nodded.

"Then why don't you finish it for us, mister?"

"I will fear no evil: for Thou art with me."

"No, Leo," Twyla said, interrupting him. She shook her head. "He's not here with you."

"Who?" Leo said.

"God. Your evil is what you have to fear."

Keir pointed out the door and the things that chased Leo through the forest were still out there, waiting for him. "But they are here with you."

"Each one was spawned from a sin you indulged in," Twyla said. "Suppose people knew that all of their sins created those beings and that they would get a chance to get back at them for all their suffering. Do you think they'd still do it?"

Leo looked out into the deformed crowd and swallowed hard. The menacing faces wanted their revenge. Their hatred was tangible and he didn't want to see them anymore so he turned away, trying to formulate a plan of escape.

"Why do you turn your back on them like that?" Twyla said.

"Because I don't like what is see."

"That is not their fault. They're living, breathing entities that despise ever being born. Could you imagine coming into being because of someone's sins?"

He shook his head. "No, that must be terrible."

"Then you should understand why every moment of awareness for them is dedicated at getting back at you."

"I didn't know my bad decisions did that. I was sick."

"Being ignorant of the commandments doesn't exclude you from the law. You must pay for your sins by facing them. Every single one of them."

He looked over his shoulder at the group and whimpered.

"I can't do it," he said and looked at the smoldering ash inside the fireplace. There was barely a flame and the darkness outside had started to seep into the cabin.

"If you don't go, they'll come in to take you. Their time has come and they won't wait any longer. For the valley of death is inescapable."

Twyla's words had become background noise as he searched for a way out. There had to be a way. He thought about running through the library of the dead, but the idea of the mischievous imp having set an elaborate trap made him dismiss that thought. He looked some more and found his gaze going outside and drifting over the crowd and to the forest. That's when he spotted a narrow path that routed through the crowd and disappeared into the tree line. It was his only chance and he would have to move fast, but he could make it. Maybe he could lose them in the dense woodlands. Without hope, he had nothing.

"The only thing that remains now is your penance," Twyla said.

Leo studied the path some more and mapped his course. He looked at the bluish flame that flickered and threatened to quit. He needed more time. Desperate to preserve the light that was his only chance at surviving this hell, he turned his attention to the table and stools.

"If you choose to run, they will hunt you and will never tire. But if you choose to give in to them, your suffering will end much quicker than their own."

"I'm not going to lie down for them," he said, defying what was to come.

"I find it curious how people look to cling to what is left of their lives in these final moments when the fate that is in front of them is something that is inescapable. And yet during their lives, it meant nothing to waste a day."

"That's the hard part about being human," Leo said. "Hating what you have and hoping for a better tomorrow that never comes. We don't know any better so what do we have to compare it to?"

"To them," Twyla said, and pointed outside.

"No," he said, and shook his head. "If people knew this was what their sins created and this was what they had to face, then they wouldn't do it."

"Only it doesn't work that way. People behave freely, thinking consequences will never catch up to them. Like you did."

"And I can't go back to tell myself not to do it? To change my ways?"

"You had your chances, Leo. It's time."

"Well you can't expect me to just give up!"

Leo lifted a barstool and smashed it on the floor, breaking it into pieces. He tossed the wood onto the fire.

"What are you doing?"

"Trying to survive."

The wood quickly took a flame and pushed the darkness back.

"No, no, no!" Twyla shouted. "You can't do that!"

"What do you think you're doing, mister?" Keir said and hurried into the dark room.

"What does it look like I'm doing?" Leo said and grabbed a chair leg, removed his shirt, and wrapped it around the end. Tying it tight, he touched the shirt to the flames and watched the fire engulf the fabric. Just then, Keir came back into the room and Leo turned away, his lit torch spewing black soot into the air. Water splashed over the fire and hot embers hissed, belching steam up the chimney.

"Now get out, mister," Keir said and dropped the empty bucket onto the floor. "You're more trouble than you're worth."

As fast as he could, Leo ran out of the cabin and the things stepped back, trying to avoid the firelight. Disappearing into the forest, the pack howled and gave chase.

23

CONSEQUENCES OF DECISIONS

The past.

Sparks of pain coursed through Leo's body and he gasped for breath. Hot, searing agony exploded from his gut and he remembered the knife and how it had sunk deep inside his belly. Heat spilled out of his body and he looked at Saint Nick as he twisted the knife around. Suspended in the grasp of two faceless men who stood behind him, there was something incredible about this moment. That voice, the one that told him what to do, was gone, stifled by the sharp blade.

"You come here with your accusations," Saint Nick said, his voice coming from a blackness that filled Leo's vision. "You've been trying to keep up with this lie you've wrapped yourself in but this time you've gone too far. It's time you went and joined your momma. I hope she gets her chance to confront you."

Those words hurt, but Leo's physical pain far exceeded it. His body stiffened as he tried to resist what he now thought were hands pulling out the insides of his body. Then he fell to the ground. Or was he falling through it?

"I'm sorry, Mom," he mumbled, and a metallic taste filled his mouth. He spit blood.

"Leo?" a voice of concern said.

A pitch black veil approached and threatened to cover him but he tried to turn away from it and follow the voice. But the voice sounded far away and he couldn't see anything but shadows that morphed. His head throbbed something awful, competing with the ache in his abdomen.

"Wendell, call nine-one-one and tell them someone has been stabbed," the voice said.

"Pastor," Leo tried to say but could only manage an incomprehensible wheeze.

Leo listened to footsteps quickly fading down the alleyway and splashing through puddles. A deformed face distressed with pain pushed out of the darkness and snarled at Leo. It tried to break free of the tendrils that bound it but it was pulled back in, screams fading into the bleakness.

A chill settled deep in Leo's bones and numbed his skin. Shivering, he could do nothing but concentrate on the pain that ripped at his insides and hope that the black didn't spew anything else.

"You should mind your own damn business, preacher man."

The sound of Saint Nick's voice called Leo out of the darkness. He forgot about his pain for a moment and wanted to get up and tell him to leave the pastor alone, that he was the only thing good in a constant state of bad.

"He deserves what he got," Saint Nick said. "He's a junkie and he killed his own mother. How can he be saved from that?"

"Is that true, Leo?" the preacher said.

Leo couldn't muster the strength to say it.

"I don't know how you think someone like him could be saved," Saint Nick said.

"I do the work of the Lord and that is having mercy upon His sheep."

"You should move your business, preacher man, or you'll be next."

"I don't fear your impious ways, son. I've come here to challenge them in the name of the Lord."

"The people you're looking to save don't want your help. And I don't think one of them is worth the life of that boy who just ran out of this alleyway."

"Lead me not into temptation," the preacher said. "But deliver us from evil."

"You keep that in mind, preacher."

"For thine is the kingdom and the power and the glory."

Leo felt the warmth of hands press down on him. They provided him with comfort, and they also worked to stop the bleeding. But he knew the laceration was far too deep and had mangled his innards beyond repair. He gathered the strength to lift his icy hand and place it on top of the pastor's hand.

"I am here with you, Leo," Pastor Grant said.

"I have a confession to make, preacher man," Saint Nick said with a laugh. "I killed a man today and seek forgiveness."

"Confess your sins, Leo," the pastor said, ignoring Saint Nick. "Have remorse and ask for forgiveness."

But it was too late. The darkness in front of Leo wrinkled, making way for a white hand, dotted with age spots. It reached for him and took his hand, tugging him into the void.

"As I walk through the valley of shadow of death, I shall fear no evil," the pastor said. "For Thou art with me; thy rod and thy staff they comfort me."

"Run, Leo," a terrible voice said, and the hand that guided him let him go and he fell. The smell of wet dirt and rotting foliage filled his nostrils and something ominous made him stand. He stood in a darkened forest, confused at how he got there, distracted by whatever was around him because it felt malicious and alive.

He saw an opening in the thick foliage and ran as fast as he could.

BOOKS BY
KEITH ROMMEL

Shade of the Reaper Series
The Cursed Man
The Lurking Man
The Sinful Man
The Silent Woman

Devil Tree Series
The Devil Tree
The Devil Tree II

The White River Monster
Ice Canyon Monster